calling out

A NOVEL BY RAE MEADOWS

calling out

A NOVEL BY RAE MEADOWS

MacAdam/Cage

MacAdam/Cage
155 Sansome Street, Suite 550
San Francisco, CA 94104
www.macadamcage.com

Library of Congress Cataloging-in-Publication Data

Meadows, Rae.
  Calling out / by Rae Meadows.
     p. cm.
  ISBN 1-59692-165-X (alk. paper)
  1. Young women—Utah--Salt Lake City—Fiction. 2. Escort serv-
ices—Utah—Salt Lake City—Fiction. 3. Utah—Fiction.
I. Title.
  PS3613.E15C36 2006
  813'.6—dc22

                                        2006000699

"Come Rain or Come Shine" Music by Harold Arlen. Words by
Johnny Mercer. ©1946 (Renewed) Chappell & Co. All Rights
Reserved. Used by Permission.

Manufactured in the United States of America.
10 9 8 7 6 5 4 3 2 1

Book and jacket design by Dorothy Carico Smith.

For APD

The conformity we often glibly equate with mediocrity isn't something free spirits "transcend" as much as something they're not quite up to.

—Peter De Vries, *The Tents of Wickedness*

chapter 1

It's the taxidermist. I can tell by my caller ID. His picture, which he once gave to one of the girls, is taped to the wall above my phone, between a photocopy of our business license and the list of descriptions that Mohammed has written to help sell the girls: "classy, mature, enthusiastic, efervessent, exotic, curvie"—whatever adjective might get a caller going.

The taxidermist lives down in Nephi, a town named for the righteous, fair-skinned leader of an ancient Hebrew tribe who, the Book of Mormon claims, brought his followers to America by boat in 600 B.C. But this modern Nephi doesn't offer much more than windy, lonely scrub hills. It's the sticks, even for Utah.

The taxidermist pays a $300 travel fee for a girl to drive three hours there and three hours back. That's on top of the $120 per hour he pays for the time she spends with him, not including a usually good-sized tip.

In the photograph, his hands are on his hips and his

feet are apart, as if he's just quelled an uprising. He's wearing a long denim coat with epaulettes and leather lapels. His hair hangs just past his shoulders, frizzed and bleached yellow with dark roots and lifted up and away from his face by a breeze. He's thirtyish, with a gut, and I can picture him in the cab of his pickup with the rigid legs of a stuffed deer sticking up behind him. The hunter. The craftsman. Sure of his manly role in the world. The photo was posted as a joke but its continued display is evidence of his mascotlike status among us.

His name is Ephraim and sending him an escort is a lengthy process. He claims he doesn't like anyone who's available, he gets surly about the last girl he saw, he haggles over the travel fee. But Ephraim in Nephi doesn't have a wealth of romantic options, so eventually he'll say okay, and sigh, as if he's doing everyone a favor by letting a girl come to him. He treats all of us—the phone girls, the escorts, probably even the woman at the drive-through window—as if we conspire against him.

The escorts complain that he trumpets his skill as a taxidermist, that he reeks of formaldehyde, that he reminds every girl she is lucky to have been chosen. But after paying out to the house and tipping the booker, the girl takes home about $500 for just three hours of face time, which makes even Ephraim worth the trip. Plus he gives each of his female visitors the souvenir of a fox pelt, which I find endearing.

The last time I talked to Ephraim, I pitched him Sunshine, one of our older girls, describing her as thirty, blond, a class act. Actually she's in her early forties and, though pleasant, not exactly cheerful, especially given her ragged-edged smoker's voice. She is blond, though, and that's usually all that matters. Booking an escort requires a few bets to be hedged, a little confidence, and a glimpse of insight into the mind-set of a man who calls an escort service from the barren middle west of Utah. Ephraim is, like most callers, nothing if not optimistic, and that night the blond hair conjured enough sexiness for him to imagine a fulfilling evening.

But the feeling of erotic promise shrivels quickly in a one-sided endeavor. Apparently Sunshine didn't know what a taxidermist was when she agreed to head to Nephi. She barreled into the office at five o'clock the following morning, still mad after three hours on the road, insisting she would never see that disgusting son-of-a-bitch again. When she slammed the office door on her way out, I couldn't help but imagine the slamming door of Ephraim's workshop, and then the sound of the doleful Nephi wind, as he found himself, once again, alone.

But the taxidermist always calls again. And tonight, I'm almost glad he has. It's a rule that we don't let the men know we have caller ID—this business is all about mystique, Mohammed tells us—so I pretend I don't know it's him and I start from the beginning.

"Good evening, this is Roxanne. How may I help you?"

"It's Ephraim," he says.

Like all regular callers, he assumes an air of entitlement. He expects me to know him and to show deference. I'm supposed to ask if he's used our service in the last six months and to recite the "Utah rules" so there are no misunderstandings. But I know this will make him angry, so I don't. Most regulars shed all embarrassment, any hint of shame—many become self-righteous. But there is something about Ephraim, a naked desperation in his voice he can't fully conceal, that makes me want to cheer him up.

"Have you see Nikyla before?" I ask. There are four girls on the schedule, but none of them has called in.

"Sounds foreign," Ephraim complains.

"It's just an exotic name. I think you'll really like her."

"I want real tits. None of them fake ones. And not one of those kids, neither. They don't know how to act," he says.

"She's twenty-four, 5'4", 110 pounds, 34D-24-34, long black hair and green eyes. A stunning beauty. The most amazing breasts. Real and full. You won't believe how luscious they are," I say, "You'll think you're dreaming."

The only thing I'm lying about is that Nikyla is barely nineteen, but she is more mature and self-possessed than her age might suggest. Ephraim takes the bait.

I have to page Nikyla a few times before she calls me back, but she agrees to see Ephraim because she likes me and because she wants to get away from her boyfriend's mother who's going on and on about the Mormon president's exalted General Conference address. Nikyla has never gone to see the taxidermist but she laughs when I tell her who it is and says it's sort of like winning a fucked-up lottery. Ephraim may be the butt of our jokes but he is so heartbreakingly fallible we treat him with a certain gentleness. Because I know what he looks like, the longing on the other end of the line is all the more palpable. I imagine him answering the phone in his cold metal shed, surrounded by glass eyes and mounted elk heads with their antlers not yet sewn into place.

"Hello, Ephraim, it's Roxanne from Premier," I say.

"Yeah," he says.

"Nikyla is on her way."

"Better be. I don't got all night."

"Ephraim, sweetie," I say, my voice a slow, aural smile that melts the border between reality and fantasy, "You have a happy Thanksgiving."

*

In the spring of 1846, Brigham Young set off for the Rockies with 70 wagons carrying 143 men, 3 women, 2 children, a boat, a cannon, 93 horses, 55 mules, 17 dogs, and some chickens. I left Manhattan on a warm May day with everything I owned either crammed into my old Subaru wagon or piled high on top like the shell of a turtle, and I drove west on Highway 80 with little more to direct me than an *Outside* magazine article about the high quality of life in a city surrounded by mountains in the valley of the Great Salt Lake. I had faith in the curative power of new geography. Brigham Young had stopped his wagon train at the mouth of Emigration Canyon and said, "This is the place," and so would I.

There was the fetid lake smell but I grew used to it soon enough. And the Mormon cultural oddities, like excessive politeness and proud moral correctness and 3.2 beer, I found refreshingly quaint. Even the missionaries were amiable when I lied and told them I was Jewish to make them go away. Besides, no one knew me in Salt Lake City and it was a long way from New York, which made it as good a place as any.

My real name is Jane. I've lived in Utah for six months. My landing here may seem random, but I like to think that there was some sort of fatalistic breeze that steered me to this place. Although I don't have a particular sense that the land of Zion is where I'm supposed to be, I do feel at ease here. The landscape hasn't yet been dulled by the patina of disappointment.

chapter 2

Even phone girls need pseudonyms for safety and, I realize now, to make a game of the whole thing. It took me a few times before I could say "This is Roxanne" without laughing. Kendra did phone sex before working here, so she is all seduction, all business. She holds a Benson & Hedges 100 between crimson, acrylic-nailed fingers and books more dates than anyone. She says it's about fore-play. I see it more as straight sales. Bait and switch. Leads and closing. Either way, it comes down to the fact that we're paid to prey on men's desire and loneliness.

Most of our clientele are local and they've used us before. But some are just in town for business.

"We are a legal escort agency," I say in a low flirty voice. "There is no sexual contact involved. I can send a lovely young lady to see you, she can dance, do a little striptease…"

I trail off to be suggestive, because other than sexual contact, what an escort and client can do is limited only by their own creativity. But with the out-of-towner I'm usually met with the standard disbelief, the insistence on how the "no sex" part can't possibly be true. I didn't believe it either when I answered the classified ad for a phone manager, but the job's legality did make it easier for me to justify taking it. "Here at Premier," Mohammed told me then in his guttural Arabic accent, "we do things by the book and with integrity." And the Utah men keep coming back.

In the Premier lounge hangs a poster with a climber gripping an impossibly sheer rock face. In bold script beneath the image it says, "Strive for Excellence!" On the wall of the bathroom in a scratched plastic frame is a list titled "Reasons Not to Break the Law." Number ten reads, "Your self-esteem will suffer—who wants to be a whore!" With that exclamation point I always read the last clause as a cheer. Mohammed composed this list to keep his young charges in line, to simplify the Byzantine maze of regulations and codes to which Utah-style escort services are subject. A few months ago he had to pay a fine for an escort who encouraged an undercover officer to mastur-bate while he watched her. This was after he had her lick chocolate from his inner thighs, which is perfectly legal.

Since I'm not from Utah, I volunteered to work this shift so the other phone girls could spend Thanksgiving with their families. I told my parents I wasn't coming home to Ohio because I had to finish an important project—they think I work at a small advertising agency—but really I didn't want to have to face too many questions about what I'm up to in Utah. My sister will be there with her husband and in-laws, which stressed my mom out enough that she didn't press for my attendance.

I used to love Thanksgiving, the consistency and ritual of it, the forest green cloth napkins, the good silverware, the overdone turkey, my mom's earnest blessing, our required pronouncements of the things we were thankful for. But at some point my sister and I no longer had much to say to each other, and my dad grew quiet, and Thanksgiving became more of a duty than anything else. Last year, my sister was with her husband's family, so it was just the three of us. My mom didn't ask me to help mash the potatoes or set the table. Instead we had dinner at the country club.

Tonight the heater comes on only intermittently and the cable is out altogether. I've been scraping ancient Scotch tape remnants from the desk in between reading sections of a month-old Sunday *New York Times*.

Mohammed rushes in to drop off some new invoice sheets, chattering in Arabic on his cell phone with barely a nod hello in my direction. He's in his fifties, his hair still inky-black, and though he says he's 5'9", so am I, and he's shorter than I am by at least two inches. He emerges from his office a moment later and looks over my shoulder at the night's meager phone log, then shakes his head, his cinnamon complexion gone ashy.

"Who's working?" he asks.

"Um. Nikyla's on her way to Nephi. I haven't gotten a hold of Mimi or Vivian. Or Miranda."

"So who?"

"At the moment, no one. But Jezebel's on later."

"No one?"

"No one," I say, "but it's Thanksgiving. I don't think that many people are going to call."

"Oh you don't," he says. "How am I supposed to run a business where none of the employees show up to work? They think they can just decide if they feel like working or not? These kids have no work ethic."

Mohammed also owns Saharan Sands, a Middle Eastern restaurant run by his wife, and the Carpet Oasis, an Oriental rug store, which flank the escort office. All of his businesses are losing money, so he exists in perpetual motion between the venues, on high alert for ways to turn a profit. Last month he added a belly dancer to weekend lunch and dinner hours at the restaurant. She doubles as a phone girl. He is considering a neon sign for his always-empty rug store. He had a phone line installed here for another venture, which we are told to answer by saying "Creative Artists," offering clowns, singing telegrams, and practical jokes, presumably performed by the escorts. It never rings. A French maid's costume and a musty bear suit hang in a locker in the back room.

Mohammed pulls out his cell phone but then puts it back in his jacket and begins to pace behind me. "You will have to go out," he says.

"What?"

"If someone calls and wants a date, you will have to go."

"No way," I say. "I've told you before. I don't do that."

"You don't do what? It's not sex! We're a legal business! I contributed to the mayor's campaign!"

"Mohammed," I say, "I only book the dates."

"I cannot understand you," he says, throwing his hands up. "Making money is making money. It's a service, like being a nurse or a babysitter or something like this." He rubs his temples with his eyes closed.

"I can't believe you're trying to bully me," I say. I took this job to do something different than what I knew—but not *that* different.

"If it's such a bad thing then why do you work here, huh?" But his tone betrays his resignation and he breathes out with a weary sigh.

"I'll try calling the girls again," I say.

Mohammed crosses his arms and scowls. His beeper goes off and he scurries out, leaving behind a trail of peppery cologne.

*

During my last year in New York I felt bad most of the time, seesawing between hollow numbness and a spirit-gnawing despair. It all appeared to be fine—I had a job as a successful copywriter, an underpriced rent for a sunny sublet, a screenwriter boyfriend. But I could barely haul myself up off the couch, my limbs as heavy as sodden sponges, my days increasingly enslaved by downcast ruminations about my lack of worth. I cried at TV commercials. I picked my fingers until they bled. Over that year, it became harder to ignore that, at a certain point, what I did every day defined who I was.

I'd thought that I would opt for grand experience over a regular paycheck. But I never could quite figure out what that majorly meaningful thing I should be doing was, and all of a sudden I was thirty and I'd become something that I wouldn't have imagined—I was regular. Change had happened without my consent. I stopped returning well-meaning phone calls from friends. I watched my relationship with McCallister grind down to pulp. And when he finally broke up with me, I took self-pitying pride in the totality of my failure.

One night, sometime during my fifth glass of chardonnay, I knew it was up to me to do something before bitterness enfolded me in its tough, dry shell. As I walked home from the bar, I passed downtown hipsters with their hipbones jutting above low jeans, their pricey sneakers not good for anything but hanging out. Their eyes flicked toward me as I went by but then quickly looked away. They didn't see that I was just like them. A poser. But I did.

I decided to purge my life. I gave away most of my possessions, packed my car, and moved far away from everything in an effort to give my unhappiness the slip.

*

It's nine thirty when Nikyla calls from Nephi. The girls call in on a separate phone that I know to answer immediately, no matter what.

"It's Nikyla."

"Hi. You made it," I say.

"Yep."

"Are you safe?" I ask.

If she answers yes it means she feels relatively safe and she can continue with the date. If she says no, I ask a few other yes/no questions like "Do you feel like you're in danger?" and "Can you get to the door?" and then she puts the man on the phone so I can distract him, and she gets out fast. Saying no is serious business. It isn't for being tired or grossed out or not in the mood to go through with the date.

"Yes," Nikyla answers.

"Have you collected?"

"Yes," she says again. I can picture Nikyla, all done up in a snug mandarin silk dress, and I'm glad for Ephraim.

"Okay. I'll call you out in fifty," I say. "Have fun," I add, knowing Nikyla can handle Ephraim probably better than anyone.

The phone rings again right away, but by the number I can tell it's Manny, a.k.a. Juan, a.k.a. Sam Gomez. He's on our 86ed list for writing bad checks, and even though we won't send him an escort, he often calls just to try. It makes me slightly uneasy when one of the banned guys calls. My refusals incite frustration and anger, and I fear the day one of them decides to come in here to take what he wants. The office is unmarked and nondescript, and people have to be buzzed in. Its only window is covered by large-slatted venetian blinds, and it could pass for a dentist's office were it not for the security camera poised above the door. But our address is no secret, and the camera has never been properly installed, so it's a ruse at best. I know Mohammed won't spend the money to have it repaired until something bad happens.

*

Jezebel comes in around ten and rescues me from Mohammed's badgering. Blond with transparent blue eyes, she is eighteen but she could pass for thirteen—a big hit with clients who are looking for young. She's small-boned and small-chested, and she'd seem almost elfin if not for her loud voice, brazen cheekiness, and very short, tight leather skirt. Like many of the girls, Jezebel grew up Mormon and she thought it would be funny to have a biblical pseudonym.

In one hand she has a paper plate of turkey and pumpkin pie for me, and in the other she grasps the body of her new spaniel puppy, who is trying to bite her sleeve.

"Albee is a much bigger pain than I thought he was going to be," she says. "Can he stay here when I'm out?"

Jezebel knows Mohammed would have a fit if he

found a dog in the office, no animals being one of his strict policies, but she also knows that when it comes to the girls, I'm a pushover.

"Sure," I say, because I feel guilty that she had to leave dinner with her family to go out for me into the uncharted night. "As long as he doesn't pee on the floor."

"He might, but not very much comes out," she says. "Happy turkey day. Mom got started early on the vino. Pie's pretty good, though."

I eat a slice of turkey with my fingers.

"I'm sorry you have to go out on Thanksgiving," I say.

"Don't worry about it," Jezebel says. "I could use the money. The dent in my Blazer's going to cost me five hundred bucks."

"Are you saving for school? You could probably still start in January," I say with gentle prodding.

Jezebel shrugs. She opens her compact and covers the small pimples on her forehead with matte beige powder. Albee wobbles off toward the tanning closet.

Like almost everyone at Premier, Jezebel started escorting for just a few months to make some money and figure out the next step. Maybe junior college. Maybe modeling. But getting paid in a wad of cash has rendered those notions obsolete, despite my motherly advice. She bought a car. She buys new clothes and CDs. She moved into her own apartment, but she can't save enough for rent. When bill collectors call looking for Jenna Smith, I tell them no one by that name works here.

Jezebel sits on the desk, flashing me her zebra-print underwear from beneath her skirt. Mohammed has reprimanded her for dressing too much like a slut.

"You must present yourself classy. Men don't want someone arriving who looks like a hooker. Tell them," he sometimes says to me. "Tell these girls what men are like."

His turning to me as an expert always makes me laugh. When I tell the girls that these men think they want sex but most really just want company, they usually say something like, "Yeah, whatever," or, "They just want to get off," which sends Mohammed's eyes heavenward in exasperation.

Jezebel eats a bite of pie from my plate, then a forkful of whipped cream.

"I want to get my boobs done," she says. "Miranda's cost four grand. I'm going to start saving for them."

"Why would you want to do that?" I ask. "You look great as you are. Men don't like fake ones, anyway."

"You say that but they don't really know the difference. You give them the measurements and they pick by the numbers."

"That's not true. They ask specifically for real ones. Remember Diamond's? They were like rubber balls," I say.

"I'll look more even," she says, pushing her breasts up with her hands. "And if I try to do the acting thing, I need them to compete."

"Please don't do anything until you're in your twenties," I say, as if I am so world-wise. But I'm not too worried because I'm pretty sure she won't be able to save four thousand dollars.

Jezebel was once on the *Jenny Jones* show as an out-of-control teen. Now she meets men in motel rooms for money but she tells me her relationship with her mother is much better.

Jezebel peers over my shoulder at the clipboard.

"No lonely men on Thanksgiving?" she asks. "Albee, no!"

She jumps from the desk. The puppy has chewed a hole in one of the leather loveseats.

"Nikyla's with the taxidermist," I say.

She snorts. "That guy is such a freak. I had to hang the fur he gave me out on the clothesline for a week to get that smell from it."

The fact that Jezebel once had to drive 170 miles to get naked for a strange taxidermist, and that I will send her out somewhere else to get naked again on this cold holiday night, suddenly gives me a hiccup of guilt. Something about her undisguisable youth and her unflinching approach to the world makes me more fearful for Jezebel than the others.

"I gave it to my brother's wife," she says. "She put it on the wall above the fireplace. Maybe next time I see that guy I'll bring the fur back for you so you don't feel left out."

The rumor around the office is that Jezebel will have sex for extra money. I choose not to believe it. I don't want to worry about her any more than I already do.

"Hey. How come you don't ever go out?" she asks. "You'd make more than on the phone, you know."

When you work here, it is understood that escorting is in no way in the same category as prostitution. We're an entertainment company. A legal service. The girls have to believe it and outwardly I never waver.

"You could do a bachelor party with me to start," she says. "The guys are sometimes cute. The tips are good. It'd be fun."

I feel bad about thinking it but what I don't say to Jezebel is that I'm not an escort because I'm not that desperate. Self-imposed banishment is one thing, but taking off my clothes for money is quite another.

"I'm too shy," I tell her. "It's not something I could ever do." Looking down at my modest turtleneck sweater and corduroys, it's probably not hard for her to believe.

"Albee," she says, "come here, baby. You pain in my ass." She picks up the dog and puts him in my lap. "Well. The offer stands if you ever have a change of heart."

The phone rings and Jezebel's an easy sell. She always is. She gets requested much more than other girls, which certainly supports the sex-off-the-books theory. But then again, she's young, warm, and cute.

"Don't forget Nikyla. She's probably getting the creeps right about now," she says. "That guy likes to show and tell with the dead animals. He had me take his picture naked with a stuffed mountain lion like he was fucking it."

She sprays perfume, fluffs her hair with her fingers,

and smiles, giving me a dirty grind with her narrow hips
as a farewell salute. I can barely muster a smile back. This
gesture makes her look like a six-year-old imitating something she's seen a teenager do, not knowing what it means.
I'm nostalgic for the kid she must have been, or maybe
still is.

She answers her ringing cell phone—her mother—
with rolled-eyed annoyance.

"No. I can't. Oh come on. Yeah, well fuck you too," she
says into the phone.

Jezebel waves at me as she slams the door and leaves
me alone again.

*

Every time I call an escort out at the end of a date, I
have a moment of worry until I hear her voice. Nikyla
takes four rings to answer but sounds normal and upbeat.
Ephraim will stave off another night alone with help from
a vivacious teenager who is saving up for night-school
business classes.

Unlike with Jezebel, I don't worry about Nikyla getting stuck in this lifestyle for long because escorting really
is just part of the larger plan. She doesn't get sidetracked
by spending to make herself feel better. She just got a job
at a clothing store in the mall so she won't have to declare
her escort earnings on her taxes, and she wants to have a
baby as soon as her boyfriend gets promoted to manager
at Circuit City. I told her she should try living somewhere

outside of Utah where maybe she wouldn't feel the need to start having kids so young. She just smiled when I said this, feeling sorry for me because I am thirty and single and childless.

"Having babies is what human beings are supposed to do," she said. "It's our nature. Really Rox, it's all about getting more love."

I couldn't argue with that.

With Nikyla on the road for another three hours, I have no girls on call. If Mohammed knew, he'd hop up and down like Rumpelstiltskin. I should just pack up and go home, but getting no answer at an escort agency on Thanksgiving is probably worse for a sad guy than a recorded voice saying no one is available. And it's not like I have somewhere better to be. So I embark upon some improvement projects for the office, starting with scrubbing the puppy-urine spots from the carpet.

Over the months I've been here, I've come to view this softly seedy office with affection. With the closed blinds and the dim lamplight, it always looks like it's dusk. I light the electric-purple jasmine candle on the counter, then straighten the dog-eared fashion magazines on the gold-and-glass coffee table. A dusty plastic spider plant is lodged in the corner next to the TV. After I wipe its leaves shiny, it makes a nice addition to my desk. I sink into one of the black leather loveseats and look at the pictures of "Fall on the Hudson River" on the front of the *Times* travel section.

We hadn't been dating long the first time McCallister took me up to his hometown in the Hudson Valley. We played hooky on an October Tuesday and left the city behind. The day was luminous, and in a borrowed car outside our usual turf, we were smiley and shy, laughing at everything. I told him that when I was young my mom used to say to me and my sister with reverent breathiness on particularly brilliant blue-skied afternoons, "Remember this day, girls!" I imitated her with exaggerated flourish to undermine the sincerity of the sentiment, but savoring the day was exactly what I wanted to do. I felt full and solid, and humbled by possibility. Now I wonder if being happy with someone is really just stringing enough of these shiny moments together.

Three and a half years of stilted commitment later, McCallister declared an end to our relationship, citing, as he put it, our pathological disconnectedness. I feigned agreement and acceptance, even as inwardly I was devastated, and even as he started dating an actress named Maria a week later. We still talk, but the distance and my rule that I never call him make it feel like a safe arrangement. He likes to call and tell me what I'm missing in New York. He feels some kind of duty to convince me to move back though I'm not sure what for since he insists it's not for him.

The phone rings, and as I reach for it I knock over the candle, singeing a black spot on the carpet even larger than the one Albee left. The caller ID reads, "Penitentiary."

I hesitate. Sometimes when it's not busy I'll answer these calls and proceed as if they are potential clients. It's not a lot, but it's what I can offer. Tonight I appreciate the diversion, so I answer and describe Nikyla and Jezebel and Mimi and Vivian and Miranda in glowing detail. Albee wrestles with a purple satin pillow he found under the couch.

"What about you, Roxanne? You sound real nice," the caller says.

I smile and feel my lonesomeness fade just a bit.

"Sure. I go out," I say. "I don't know if I'm your type, though."

"I bet you are. Why don't you describe what you look like?"

I don't tell him that my body is long and reedy, my eyes amber-brown, my hair walnut-colored and just past my shoulders, my skin as pale as parchment. Instead I peer down at the model on the cover of *Glamour*.

"I'm twenty-two. 115 pounds. About 5'6", with honey-blond hair—"

"Is it long?"

"Long and silky. Down to the curve of my back," I say, "and I have green eyes—"

"I bet you have some cute freckles across the bridge of your nose."

"How'd you know that?"

He laughs.

"I'm a 36-24-36 with full, real breasts."

"Oh," he sighs. "I'll take you."

"What would you like me to wear tonight?"

"A short little skirt with some of those fishnet stockings. I bet you have a pair of legs on you." He whistles softly. "And wear some real sexy high spiked heels."

"I think that can be arranged," I say. "What else?"

"Tell me what your tits are like," he says, his breathing getting heavy, his voice louder and forceful.

I weigh the option to continue, seduced by his urgency and my own longing to lose myself. But then a voice in my head says, "Who *are* you?" I know it's time to cut this short. Even I recognize that keeping the charade going would be a momentary salve at best, one that would make me feel worse in the end.

"You have yourself a good night," I say, keeping the purr in my voice.

"What? Oh come on. We're just getting started."

"I'm sorry, baby. I have to go now," I say.

I hear him say "Wait," as I hang up.

And I'm alone again. The heater creaks and whistles as it pumps dry, hot air into the room.

It is three a.m. and I'm gritty-eyed and worn out. I have two hours to go. I don't want to think about anything, especially myself. I restock the invoices. I clean lint from the pen drawer. I copy over Mohammed's escort schedule for the week so it's legible. But the heater clicks off, leaving cold, early-morning silence, and I realize that I've forgotten something.

"Albee?" I call.

I stop to listen for him but the office is quiet. West of town, the Union Pacific sounds its horn and I wait a second before looking for the puppy. I close my eyes and feel the rumbling.

chapter 3

Nikyla, still amazingly peppy at the end of the night, returns from her date with the taxidermist and throws a silver fox pelt at me with a scream as if it were alive. She is not, as I had imagined, in a Chinese silk dress, but instead she's done up nicely in black velvet pants and a charcoal sweater, her cleavage barely beckoning from the V neck-line. Not even yet twenty, Nikyla seems to have it much more together than I do. She counts out money for the house with purpose and focus and then gives me two twenty-dollar bills.

"That's too much," I say. "Take half back."

"Stop. He tipped big," she says, pulling her long black hair into a ponytail.

She applies a sheer lip gloss—her boyfriend always waits up for her—and then waves as she trots for the door without reporting anything from the date.

Sometimes the escorts volunteer details, but part of the decorum around here is that we don't press for information that isn't offered. My relationship with the girls overrides my curiosity for salacious tidbits. They will talk about the fetishists because they find the strange obsessions funny and nonthreatening, and because, I assume, satisfying these men doesn't seem degrading in a way that pleasing the average john, with all his universally base urges, might.

Mark Benson calls once every other month to request an escort with long hair. He is the prize date whom the booker grants to a favorite girl because he pays $120 to brush an escort's hair for an hour, with all her clothes on and without her having to say a word. While she sits on the bed, he runs the hairbrush softly from the top of her head down through her hair with a hypnotic rhythm. Then there is Stephen Newhouse, who sits in his Corvette while an escort in a miniskirt walks back and forth in front of the car in a grocery store parking lot. And Vernal Shepherd, who takes his escort to the mall so she can model clothes for him, which he then buys for her.

But these are the exceptions. There is also the trucker who hasn't bathed in three days. The aggressive, fundamentalist Mormon venting his repressed rage. The obese shut-in who wants a body massage. The frat boys on a ski trip who've been up for two days doing coke and expect the kind of orgy they've seen in a porn video. The walleyed dentist who likes his buttocks licked. I marvel at the escorts' courage to face down another hotel room door.

My shift finally grinds to its conclusion at five a.m. and

in a sleepy stupor I drive through the early-morning-empty streets toward the Avenues, where I live, with Albee mewing on the seat next to me. After the slight panic over his earlier disappearance, I eventually found him asleep in one of the lockers in the back room, on top of a crumpled blue latex bodysuit, which he had chewed and clawed to ribbons.

By the time I get home, the ascending sun haloes the Wasatch Mountains and my frosty breath hangs in the morning air. I work my key into the door only to discover that it's unlocked.

Inside my apartment, I'm barely surprised by the tow-headed figure buried in a sleeping bag at the foot of the couch. Ford. He has my other key. His appearance is a welcome surprise; he wasn't due in for another couple weeks. I go into my room, draw all the blinds against the insistent morning, and sleep.

*

When I wake up a few hours later, I quickly splash my face with water—disheartened by the bags under my eyes—and brush my teeth before going out to greet my houseguest.

Ford and I have known each other for twelve years. We met in college, fooled around a few times, and then became friends. His baby-blond hair and small features give him an aura of innocence, though I know better. For half the year he's a river guide in southern Utah where he keeps a shingled trailer perched on the edge of a dry gulch in Moab. The rest of the time he paints houses wherever they need painting. Even though he hasn't lived in California for years, his beachy, laid-back aura is something that's as integral to him as his butterscotch-leather, worn-hard, resoled Frye boots. Proximity to Ford is one of the reasons I have stayed in Utah. Someday we might even decide that we found what we were looking for at eighteen, but I keep that inchoate nugget snuggly tucked away with my other unexamined rainy-day potentials such as journal writing, motherhood, and learning to play the harmonica.

"Morning," Ford says as I walk in to the living room.

He's propped up against the couch but still bundled in his sleeping bag, watching Martha Stewart on TV. He sips tea from a mug that says "AMF Bowling," which he bought for me during his last visit, after we rooted through the housewares at Deseret Industries, the Mormon thrift store. Albee is nosing around Ford's used tea bag, which soaks through the front page of yesterday's *Salt Lake Tribune* fanned out on the floor.

"Can I make you some?" Ford asks, holding up his mug.

"No thanks," I say. "I need coffee." I kiss the top of his head; his dirty-hair smell is boyish and familiar.

"You must have come in from the river early."

"Yep. Snow broke and the season abruptly ended. What time did you get in last night?"

"Five," I say.

He whistles. "The life of a sex worker. When did you get this guy?" he asks, lifting the puppy in one hand.

"I just kept him for the night as a favor." It's then that I notice the sleeping bag shift and a slender female arm hook over Ford's waist.

"Hey, Jane. Did I tell you I have a girlfriend?" he asks.

I look at him through narrowed eyes. "Is she of age?" I ask quietly.

Ford is famous for young girlfriends who didn't graduate from high school and who have a child or an obsessed ex.

"A very-sound-sleeping twenty-seven. Her name's Ember. You'll like her. She's a cocktail waitress in Moab but she wants to go to art school and paint. She has those kind of eyes that say 'I could have anyone in the room but I choose you.'"

"What kind of eyes are those?" I ask.

"Generous."

"Ford. You're so easy." I brush away my jealousy as if it's an errant strand of spider web, annoyed at myself for its very existence.

I motion toward the TV.

"What's she making?"

He shrugs. "You look good, Jane."

"Thanks," I say, not believing him.

"I got a job at the last minute working on a house in town. It starts tomorrow. Crack of dawn," he says. "Do you think we could stay with you for a while?"

"Sure. Of course. As long as she's neater than you are."

"I mean like a month."

"A month? Both of you?"

"Well, yeah."

My stomach retracts with instinctual opposition.

"Can we talk about this later? I'm late and I need to shower," I say. From the window the sky is slate-colored and blotchy.

Ford waves at me with one of Albee's paws as I retreat.

*

Mohammed's bronze Jaguar is parked out in front when I arrive at the office. Although I wouldn't normally have to work on a day following a night shift, I switched with Kendra—whose seasoned phone technique Mohammed pesters me to learn from—so she could take her kids camping in Little Cottonwood Canyon for the weekend. Marisa has been here since I left this morning, and from here she goes next door to belly dance at the restaurant.

"Slow?" I ask.

"Very. Mimi's at the Motel 6 by the airport. I can stay and call her out if you want."

"Don't worry about it. I'll leave you the tip in the safe."

"Thanks, Roxanne. Mohammed's at the store but I'm sure he'll be by in a few."

Marisa takes her dance costume from the hanger and unhooks her bra under her shirt. The outfit she wears to dance in looks like an armored bikini top and a brocade skirt from a community production of *Ben Hur*. She whips off her shirt and ties the top behind her back; the flesh bulges around the string. I haven't seen her belly dance, but Mohammed claims she has impressive hip isolation.

"Oh, look out for that guy from Weber who kept calling last week. The one who wants a large black girl. He starts saying nasty things after a minute or two. His number's on the clipboard," she says.

Marisa sprays perfume across her puckered abdomen. Her hair, gray rooted and reaching her waist, brushes my face as she turns to leave.

"Hello, how may I help you?" I ask, answering the phone.

"I gained at least six pounds last night. My dad had to pull me off the trough of candied yams."

McCallister.

"Where are you?" I ask.

"I just got back into the city," he says.

I imagine his wind-ripened cheeks. Even though our continued contact may be unwise, I'm glad it's him. There's a certain pleasure for me in familiar sadness, like picking a scab just to make sure it still hurts.

"How's business?" McCallister asks.

"Not a lot of callers today."

"Too many wives to visit?"

"Can you believe I worked here on Thanksgiving?" I ask, trying to make him feel responsible in some oblique way.

"It's not exactly shocking, Jane. Knowing you, I bet

you offered. Were you okay there all alone?" he asks.

"Sure. It wasn't as depressing as you might think. Did what's-her-face go upstate with you?" I ask, knowing full well that she didn't.

"She went to see her parents in San Francisco."

"How are things?" I ask, not wanting to know. We bat about the safe banter like two cats with a ball of yarn.

"Good. Really good, actually."

There is something about the way he says "really." I feel a swirling in my stomach and I want to hang up.

"Maria's moving in," he says.

The news hits me like a medicine ball in the gut. I inhale with difficulty. My eyes sting in their efforts to stay dry.

"What?" he asks. "I lost you for a second."

"Nothing," I say, "I have to go."

"Are you okay?"

"Yeah," I say. "I just have to get the other line."

"Hey," he says, "Happy Thanks—"

All those years and he never asked me to move in. Of course I never asked him either, but he's only been dating Maria for six months.

*

Mohammed returns from the rug store in a lather about a sale that didn't materialize.

"She said she wanted to buy it. She came to look at it twice. Then today she says it's not quite right. These Mormons. I don't understand them," he says, lifting his hands and letting them fall back to his sides with exaggerated theatricality.

"Maybe it had nothing to do with her being Mormon," I say. "Maybe she wasn't even Mormon."

He stops and puts his hands in the pockets of his blazer.

"Why are you so, how do you say, against the grain?" he asks.

"Because I was here all night."

There is a faint, unfamiliar knock on the front door. Mohammed looks up from rubber-banding bills together as I buzz the door open.

The woman who makes her timid entrance is in her late twenties, a shade heavy around the middle, dressed like she is interviewing for an administrative assistant position at a real estate office. She wears a boxy, shoulder-padded jacket and matching skirt, ill-fitting but neatly pressed, and a floral scarf knotted around her neck. But it's the chipped fuchsia nail polish and heavy lipstick that hint at the motivation for her appearance on this post-Thanksgiving afternoon. That, and the folded classified section of the newspaper tucked under her arm. She stops just inside the door.

"I'm here about the ad?" she says as if it's a question. She laughs, not quick enough with her hand to cover her crooked front teeth. "I saw it earlier this week but with the holiday and all. I mean it said women between eighteen and forty? It didn't say any other requirements, so, I don't know. I thought that, well, I thought maybe people look for all different types."

Mohammed signals her to step in from the door. "Come in, please. Come in. What's your age?"

"Twenty-six," she says. She appears to suck in her stomach when she says this.

Mohammed openly looks her up and down as if appraising a used car.

"Complete an application and then we'll talk," he says. "I'll be next door."

I hand her a clipboard holding a badly mimeographed application, and a pen with a mismatched top. The toilet runs loudly.

"Fill out both sides and feel free to ask me any questions," I say with a smile.

I know she is probably feeling sick about what she's doing. On closer inspection I notice a smudge on her jacket and threads hanging at the hem of her skirt. She sits on the edge of the couch and chews the inside of her cheek as she scans the sheet. The exposed need of new applicants is hard for me to witness. I want to tell her that she shouldn't do this, that she won't make it long, that her unquiet eyes give her away. But who am I to say anything.

"So on this number three," she asks, "is it really true? I don't have to go naked?"

This one gets them every time. Mohammed says to say yes because he knows they'll warm up to it when it becomes a question of money.

"It's true, technically. You don't have to do anything

you don't want to do. But I have to tell you, most clients are looking for more for their money. And the tips are higher." I feel like I'm apologizing.

When she finishes, she hands me the clipboard and cracks her knuckles. She stands near the desk, clutching her purse for security. Her face is determined and less young-looking than I'd thought at first. I see that her name is Megan but I don't read anything else to spare her the embarrassment from obvious lies about weight and body measurements.

"Do you like working here?" Megan asks.

"Yeah," I answer, "it's not so bad." And despite my conflicted feelings about this place, I mean it.

"That's nice," she says.

"I need to take your picture," I say.

"What?" She blanches.

"Oh, don't worry. Just right here. In what you're wearing. So we remember what you look like."

She straightens her shoulders and smiles with closed lips. The Polaroid is unforgiving. In the photo she looks like she's going to the prom alone in a secondhand dress. I staple her picture to her application and ring Mohammed at the rug store so he can give her the speech about how escorting is not prostitution.

"No blow jobs or hand jobs, no matter how much money," I hear him tell her, as I have heard him say to so many interviewees, including me.

When I applied, the strangeness and mystery of being

inside a dim and bedraggled escort agency had me nervous and sweating. I answered the ad because I wanted the challenge of unfamiliar territory, but as I waited, I almost lost my resolve, imagining how easy it would be for me to get a regular office job. It was only when I went back to Mohammed's office and he launched into a monologue about legal escorting that I started to relax. His accent softened the crassness of the content by giving it a clinical distance, and his animated up-and-down gesture that accompanied "hand job" I found oddly stripped of vulgarity. The only time he had nothing to say was when I told him he wouldn't have to loan me the money to pay for the license that even phone girls need one to work here. I could still afford what amounted to little more than I had paid last year for a pair of silver sandals I never wore.

Megan doesn't know it, but she is lucky Mohammed's talking to her. The girls not attractive enough get a "We'll call you" or "Get licensed and come back and see us," when Mohammed knows full well they don't have the money to get licensed or they never would have answered the ad. The truly hopeless ones, addicts or runaways or streetwalkers, haggard and rabbit-eyed, are the saddest to watch walk away.

Mohammed appears from his office.

"Go measure her. And see what she looks like with no clothes on," he says. "I can't tell what her figure is like in that matronly outfit."

"I'll measure her, but I won't have her strip," I say.

This is an ongoing battle. He keeps asking and I keep refusing. Even he, out of some sense of civility, won't go so far as to request to see an applicant in the nude, so he asks the phone girls to do it for him. The other two find a perverse sense of power in sizing up new escorts, even though neither Kendra, the ex-phone-sex worker who is fifty pounds overweight, nor Marisa, the belly dancer who is forty-five, could be an escort at Premier even if she wanted to. I tell Mohammed it isn't part of the job and it makes me uncomfortable.

"She'll have to get naked in front of the men. At least you won't be touching yourself under the covers."

"Sorry, Mohammed," I say, "No dice."

"Then just her boobs and her tummy. She says she exercises but she looks bumpy."

The phone rings.

"You're on your own," I say before answering.

He must be in good spirits because he decides to loan Megan the $250 to get licensed with the Salt Lake City Police Department. Although he only makes this offer when he thinks a girl has potential, he's always looking for the next moneymaker and he's not the best judge of a good bet. I'm amazed by Mohammed's unfettered optimism. Behind his desk is a pile of dusty VCRs and CD players, useless collateral he's accepted over the years for loans never repaid. Last week he got saddled with a snowboard.

For her collateral, Megan puts up a gold bracelet that she says came from her grandmother. She ceremoniously unclasps it from her wrist and lets go of it in Mohammed's palm with stoic deliberateness. He scribbles an illegible loan transaction record on a yellowed receipt pad and hands her the carbon copy before leaving for the restaurant. I write out a check to the city for her mandatory health check. Even though legal escorting means no sex, the city requires a full gynecological exam to check for sexually transmitted diseases. Anything, I gather, to add to the unpleasantness of the process. One more way station where the girl might still turn around and realize that the escort industry, although legal, is still sinful. But I don't think the health check will be enough deterrence for Megan.

Ford arrives just as she is leaving the office. Assuming that he is a client, she darts out the door with her head down, disappearing into the shocking glare of mid-afternoon desert sun. He looks disappointed. Despite his manly avocations, Ford is unabashedly romantic. He sees escorts as wayward nymphs waiting to be saved.

"A new applicant," I say.

"I imagined them differently," he says. "More vulnerable or something."

"She's plenty vulnerable," I say.

"You know what I mean."

"Younger and prettier," I say.

"Maybe that," Ford says. "Are you the only one here?"

"Yeah. Mohammed's next door."

"The puppy's in the car," he says.

"Oh, God. I totally forgot. You can leave him with me. Jezebel should be here soon."

Ford picks up the binder and reads the list of girls' descriptions.

"Sorry I didn't ask you before about staying. I mean, for so long. And with Ember. It all happened pretty fast," he says.

There is knock on the outside door and I buzz it open. It's Nikyla. In jeans and no makeup, her long hair down, she looks like the coed she should be.

"Hey, did you find my cell phone charger?" she asks, flipping her sunglasses up onto her head.

"Nope," I say.

"Hi," she says to Ford, "I like your boots."

In full thrift-store attire he looks a little like Jon Voight from *Midnight Cowboy*. Ford smiles. Or more accurately, he beams.

"Thanks," he says.

"Keep it together, Ford," I say.

"See you tonight, Rox," she says.

"Rox?" Ford says, eyebrows raised.

"Roxanne. My escort name."

"Nice," he says.

Nikyla gives Ford one last sideways smile and exits, sashaying out the door. He tips a nonexistent hat in her direction.

*

My shift is almost over. Jezebel picked up Albee and I am alone. I feed from a bag of Oreos Kendra has left and paint my fingernails Vamp as McCallister tells me that he thinks I'm sabotaging any chance at happiness. After our last conversation, I thought maybe I wouldn't hear from him for a while but I'm glad for the distraction. Back in New York he's looking for a winter coat.

"Remember the hookers in Paris?" he asks.

McCallister and I went to Paris a couple years ago and one day, wandering around at dusk, we came upon a strip of older prostitutes in the doorways of rue St. Denis. They were harshly made up, wrinkled and dyed, leaning with bored detachment in between grimy garment-district storefronts. Their age determined their designation to that zone, like animals let out to pasture. Their eyes were tired and lugubrious, as if they were mourning what they had once been. I went back to look at them again and again for the rest of the trip, feeling progressively worse with each visit.

"I don't get your point," I say.

"It's how you react to people around you. When you're not feeling good, you take them on. You were in a funk for the whole rest of that trip. And now you're clearly depressed."

"I'm not depressed," I say dismissively.

He guffaws but lets it go. Our conversations occupy a

delicate space, as we tiptoe around the edge of intimacy.

"Hey, what do you think about orange for a down jacket? Too flashy?" he asks.

I can hear him jostling with hangers.

"I think it's going to snow tonight," I say, "and it's not even December yet. I want it to snow. Snow is good."

"You should come back, Jane."

I wish this didn't permeate, and I'm angry with myself that it does. His words melt into my skin like balm.

"That'll surely make me happy. It worked so well before. Maybe I can hang out with you and Maria. That sounds great." I reach for another Oreo. "I wish I was one of those people who forgets to eat, like my sister. Or that I would lose my appetite when I was sad. Then at least I'd be thin."

"A) you *are* thin, and B) you just admitted that you're sad," he says. "This one isn't so bad. It fits. Do you think orange is too much? Should I play it safe with black?"

"Black is boring."

"All I'm saying, Jane, is that not being happy is sort of natural at times. It doesn't mean you should run off and hide out in the Beehive State. That is not the antidote."

"How do you know? It's not so bad here. There's plenty of parking and everyone smiles. Rent is cheap. Not everyone is cool and stylish. No roaches." I sweep cookie crumbs into a line with my finger.

I hear him ask someone the time.

"Jane? I better go. Call me if you get lonely," McCallister says.

"Go with the orange one," I say. Then, maddeningly, my voice cracks at the end of saying "good-bye."

One of the reasons I fell for McCallister was that he was nothing like my father. It didn't take me long to figure this out but there was some satisfaction in naming it. My dad, providing he has his Scotch, can sit through pork roast, mashed potatoes, and green beans, and on into coffee without saying a word. But McCallister always has something to say and this makes me feel safe. It was when he couldn't get me to say much in return, after years of coaxing, that he finally gave up. "Love," he announced one day, "is about taking that risk of losing control. And you, Jane, will not take that risk. At least not with me." He was right, but I never believed that he was taking much of a risk either. I listened. I nurtured. I made no demands. I couldn't ask for what I didn't even know I wanted. Besides, he'd already met Maria.

I blow on my nails to dry them but upon inspection they are smudged and messy around the edges so, instead, I scrape at the still-soft polish with a scissor blade. I slip, and I slice my pinkie. While foraging in the bathroom for a Band-Aid, the phone rings. I consider letting it go—there are only a few minutes left until I punch out—but as I peer around to my desk, I can see it's Scott.

Scott the contractor used to fall into the once-a-monther category. He usually calls as he's driving up from Provo to a building site when he has some time to kill. He doesn't show up on anyone's 86ed list, which means he's tolerable and not a bad tipper. Someone has penciled in on the margin of his client sheet, "handsome & sexy," and another girl wrote, "cuuuuuuuute!!!!!! nice ass!!!!!" He's been calling more frequently lately and he hasn't booked an escort for two months. I'm beginning to think he's calling for me.

When I answer, he says, "Hi, beautiful."

Despite myself—he's never seen me—I'm flattered, and I speak to him with perked-up conviviality.

"Hey Scott. How are you?"

"Just fine," he says. "Enjoying this gorgeous fall day. Driving up from Happy Valley to check in on a job. Anyone available who I might like?"

"You're in luck. I have this girl who you'll really like. Have you seen Nikyla before?"

"Doesn't sound familiar. Why don't you describe her for me," he says.

I give him the standard rundown on Nikyla that hooks everyone.

"I don't know," he says, seeming distracted, "she doesn't sound like my type."

Nikyla is everyone's type.

"So what about you, Roxanne? Do you ever go out?" he asks.

This is one of the perils of the job—phone-girl intrigue—but from Scott it does feel more substantial.

"Now, now. None of that," I say. I hope the tease in my voice belies my blush. "You know I just work the phone."

"You sure do. You have a great voice, you know. Sort

of FM-radio sultry," he says.

"Thanks," I say. "That's nice of you. Now how about Nikyla? I think you two would have fun."

"You do, huh?" Scott laughs. "She's a hair young for my taste. You sound more like what I'd like."

I fill in the letters of "handsome" on his information sheet. Under "Client Description" is written in girlie handwriting, "sandy hair, blue eyes, six feet." I imagine he has sun-squint creases around his eyes like McCallister.

"For all you know," I say, "I could be sixty and weigh three hundred pounds."

"You and I both know that's not true, Roxanne."

He says this in a way that is vaguely scolding, and despite there being no uncovered windows in the office, I have a fleeting sense of being watched.

"So maybe you'd like to see Nikyla?" I ask in a last-ditch effort to book a date, feeling like the real Jane is starting to show in my voice.

"Well," he sighs. "Unfortunately I don't have all that much time this afternoon. Unless you change your mind. I'd blow off everything for you."

I laugh, relieved, back safely entrenched behind the façade.

"It was nice talking to you, Scott," I say. I let my voice meander.

"As always," he says. "Hey, are you working tomorrow?"

I write "Yes!" on his client sheet.

"Let's just leave that as a surprise, shall we?"

chapter 4

Ford is working as part of a crew gutting a house north of
the LDS temple and on the first day he befriended Ralf, a
Mormon ex-vending machine supplier from Tooele, a
town in the desert west of Salt Lake. They spent the afternoon breaking out the windows of the house with pick-
axes, then covering them in plywood. But five minutes to
shift end, Ralf tripped on a loop of copper wire and landed
with a shard of glass in his chin. Even though I'd rather be
in bed, Ford cajoles me into joining them—post-emer-
gency room visit—at the Starlight Lounge so I can meet
both Ralf and Ember, whose face I haven't yet seen.

Ralf is attractive in a dirty Mormon kind of way. His
shaggy light hair is in a shelf cut, a sort of John Denver,
late-seventies style that half covers his ears. He looks at
home just sitting here.

"Where's Ember?" I ask.

"She went to see some friend of hers in town for the
night. You'll meet her soon, though," Ford says. "I promise."

I haven't yet told him they can stay but I know I could never tell him no.

The vinyl of the booth squeaks as Ralf scoots in to make room for me. When I sit, it feels as though roots take hold, and I sink into weariness beneath the murmuring heat pouring down from the vent above our table. Ford, his hands red-roughed and dirt-stained, slides his beer to me.

Although we are the same age, Ralf seems younger because Ford announces that he was a virgin until he was twenty-five, and also because his green eyes are so light they are almost gray, and so eager they glisten like those of a boy who has just seen his first centerfold. Ralf did his mission in Amsterdam. Although he drinks and smokes, he still believes.

"Ford tells me you came here from the big city," he says. "Why'd you leave?"

Ford leans across the table. "I'd like to hear this too."

"Because my chronic dissatisfaction made me feel middle-aged," I say, drinking three full gulps of Ford's Corona.

Ralf smiles and nods and drums his thumbs against his beer bottle. His chin is covered in a large bandage that looks like a flesh-colored beard. There is a darkened blood smear on the collar of his work shirt.

When I got out of college, I imagined myself as a Peace Corps volunteer, or a writer, or an environmental activist, or a teacher, or, for a brief phase, a midwife. But when it came down to it, I lacked passion and I was a wimp. I moved to New York because my friends did, took a job at an ad agency because it was available, spent a lot of time in bars talking about books and pop culture because that's what people did in Manhattan. I blundered through my twenties.

"It's that thing where no one can talk about anything really without irony," Ford says, near drunk. "I'm glad you got out of there, Jane."

"Pretty soon whole years passed and other people were figuring out what they were going to be when they grew up and I was still pretending I didn't have to. When really, I was becoming a loser," I say.

"Hey," Ford says quietly, "take it easy. Don't be so hard on yourself." A sheen on his expansive forehead catches the low-wattage yellow light of the bar's tavern lamps. "You should have hung out more with me out here. Drowning your sorrows in Gram Parsons," he says.

Ralf is still nodding and then wiggles his chin to get at the itch of his newly sewn wound. "Nothing wrong with Gram Parsons," he says. "I'd like to propose a toast. To Utah."

"Here, here." Ford says. "You took a long detour to get here, Jane, but I'm glad you made it."

"Aw, Ford. You old softie."

Ralf wears a broad, contented smile as he sits amidst his new friends, and he orders us another round. Ruddiness blooms in his cheeks. He licks his bee-stung bottom lip.

"So, Jane," he says. "I hear you work for a brothel."

"Not quite," I say.

"I know, I know. Tell me some stuff about it."

"What do you want to know?" I ask.

"Ford here says it's legal. But I don't know how that can be true," he says.

"There is this sheet of paper that we give all new escorts that lists what they can and can't do within the law." I lower my voice as not to attract the ears of the university students at the next table. "Can't do: sex, hand jobs, blow jobs, any touching of sexual areas, give a massage, allow or encourage masturbation."

"What? That last one seems for the birds," Ralf says, slapping his palms on the table. "Isn't that the whole point?"

"Can do," I say, "Kiss, cuddle, caress, tease, strip, take a shower, nibble on his ears, give a bubble bath, tell sexy stories, play with his nipples, sexy poses, spank, get a massage, model lingerie, talk dirty, role-play, tickle, talk about fantasies, lick chocolate off him, kiss his thighs, put on baby oil, moan and groan, tell secrets, tell jokes, dance, kiss his neck, lick his nipples, have your toes sucked, and anything else not on the can't-do list."

"Tell jokes?" This item on the list makes Ford laugh so hard he's silent and tears leak from his eyes.

"But no hugging," I say, "because a girl might press her breasts into a client, and in the eyes of Utah law, this evil far exceeds that of her having to explore the nether region of a stranger's hot and hairy inner thighs."

"That is so gross," Ralf says. He looks as if he just found out there's no tooth fairy. "So you, like, set up these rendezvous-es?"

"Yeah." I fish around in my wallet and pull out the laminated card: "Salt Lake City Sexually Oriented Business Employee, Outcall."

"Nice picture," Ralf says.

"So, Jane," Ford says, "maybe you should do it."

"What?"

"That. Try it out."

"Be an escort?"

"Yeah. Be an escort."

I laugh. "Are you serious?"

"Yeah, why not? It's legal," he says. "I assume you don't have a moral issue with it."

Ford's challenge irks me. Ralf stares first at Ford, then at me.

"Maybe it seems slightly degrading?"

"I don't know, does it? I mean is it that different from getting compensated for a bad blind date? Or being a therapist of sorts? Who's to say you wouldn't find it kind of satisfying. You go for the needy ones."

"You're drunk," I say.

"You'd be popular if you did it, though," Ralf says.

My eyes are dry and I don't have the energy to respond to either of them.

"I'm going to go," I say. "It's been a long few days."

Outside it's a bone-chilling night; the desert sky is

vast and clear. My old car creaks and coughs like a codger with emphysema until the engine catches.

*

When I arrive at the office the next day, Mohammed is already there trying to fix the perpetually running toilet.

"Did you bring toilet paper?" I ask.

"I'll bring some over from the restaurant. I can't get this stupid thing to stop," he says.

"You could call a plumber."

"Hah. That's so American. Plumbers just rip you off. I can fix this. You people don't know what hard work is."

"Yeah, tell that to the girls who have to kiss some creepy old guy who's taken out his teeth."

Mohammed emerges from the bathroom wiping his hands with a paper towel, the sleeves of his silk suit rolled up to his elbows. He has the jittery diligence of someone who has somewhere else to be.

"You always think I should feel sorry for them. Like I force them to do what they do," he says. "It's good money. It beats working three times as many hours at McDonald's, doesn't it? Or being a hooker? They're not walking State Street to get picked up by crazies and murderers. It's good money. It's legal. I file taxes."

I think that something about our ongoing antagonism helps settle any ethical dilemmas Mohammed has. And it makes me feel better too.

"But maybe if they didn't have the option, they'd go

to school or something," I say.

"You are a dreamer," Mohammed says. "You see how it all works—the way these girls like the money, why they choose to do it—but you still make believe it can be different. It is a masquerade." He rattles off something in Arabic and rolls down his sleeves. "Did you know I was going to be a doctor? I was accepted at the medical school at the University of Bologna. My father liked the idea. I might have been a good doctor, no?" His cell phone rings.

"Someday you'll tell me how you ended up here," I say.

"Okay, okay. I'll be right over," he says into the phone before flipping it closed. To me he says, "Before I forget, you have to go on a recruiting trip to American Bush."

"No way, Mohammed."

"I told you it was part of the job when I hired you. Just have a few drinks. Give out cards to the pretty dancers."

"There is no way I am doing that," I say, mortified by the notion of being a public escorting emissary.

"Tell them they'll make more money working here. Wear something classy like a suit. Twenty-five-dollar finder's fee for each one. It's a good deal for you."

I shake my head as he scuttles out the door.

The sound of rustled silk and rattled window blinds resonates until the soft insistence of the ticking wall clock reasserts itself on the room. It is noon but in the darkened office, with the candle ablaze on the counter, it could be the middle of the night.

Jezebel blows in, puppy in hand, her skirt slit up to

her underwear. She plops the dog in my lap and looks over my shoulder at the night's escort list.

"Please push me. Please, please, please? I need cash. Rent is late again. I swear, I just paid it. I don't know how it could be due already."

"I'll do my damnedest," I say, holding up my fingers in the scout's-honor position. "How's Albee?"

"I don't know what to do about him. I'm hoping my brother will take him. They already have two kids anyway, what's a dog?"

Albee clamps his teeth on my watch and I can feel his incisors against my wrist. Jezebel has disappeared into the tanning closet. I call back to her that tanning will give her wrinkles but she ignores me and the hum of the old UV lamp makes me think I'm getting my own dose of carcinogenic radiation without any of the benefits. Albee starts to pee on my leg, and before I can deposit him on the floor, the phone rings. I trade the puppy for the phone and answer without looking at the number.

"Hello, this is Roxanne. How may I help you?" I blot the warm blotch of urine on my thigh with a wad of tissues, my voice not revealing my perturbed scowl.

"Hey, beautiful. I thought you might be in. How are you today?"

Scott's intimate manner catches me off guard.

"Hi there. I'm fine, thank you. Would you like to see a lady today?"

"You know who I want to see. I was wondering if you

like to golf. We could shoot off to the driving range and hit a few balls. Then some dinner. What do you say?"

"That sounds lovely. Now I do have Jezebel today," I say.

"I'm driving up from Provo right now. I could be there in forty minutes. Come on. A late-lunch-break date."

I hope I sound cooler than I feel. I like this despite its eeriness.

"Thanks, baby, but you know I can't," I say. "Besides, I don't know how to golf." The other line rings. "Scott, hold for just a moment."

I pick up and McCallister asks, "Did I ever tell you about the time when I went home to live with my mom after I came back from Aspen? I had no money, no job, nothing to do. It was really snowy upstate that winter. I wore this bright red one-piece pajama suit every day for four months. You know the kind with the butt flap? I slept in it, then got up and did a bong hit, layered on snow clothes and shoveled obsessively. I even shoveled out the neighbors' cars. Then I'd go inside, transfer to the couch, my mom would make me nachos and hot chocolate, and we'd play Scrabble."

I see that Scott has finally tired of waiting on hold and has hung up.

"Jesus, McCallister. You must have been in bad shape," I say.

"Are you kidding? That was the best time of my life."

I hear him exhale cigarette smoke.

"Feeling nostalgic?"

"I wish I understood why I was happy then."

"You had no worries and you had limitless time-wasting activities."

"Yeah," he says, sounding flat and melancholy.

"So when's she moving in?" I ask.

"Couple weeks."

Sounds of calamitous New York City intrude through his cell phone.

"What are you doing?" I ask.

"Going to my shrink."

"Do you tell him you call me?" I ask.

"Maybe," he says. "Sometimes."

"Do you tell what's-her-face?"

"No. She wouldn't understand."

"No, I bet she wouldn't."

"How are the whores?" he asks.

"Fine," I say. "It's a slow day."

"How are you, Jane?"

"Fine."

"Fine?" he asks.

"Fine," I say.

"I think you're being aggressively distant."

"I think it might snow today," I say.

I went to a therapist for a few months a couple years ago at McCallister's urging, or more as a condition of our continued involvement. She was an older woman who worked out of her Upper East Side apartment, with soothing cream-colored carpeting, soft beige walls, and a Lithuanian doorman who used to give me a solemn smile and a slight bow because he knew who I was going to see.

I brought up my father's drinking often because I knew she liked me to talk about it. My dad is all about control and his alcohol consumption is no exception. Scotch on the rocks, his glass perpetually filled. When my dad drinks, he becomes even more reserved.

"Absent while present," the therapist said, nodding.

It's not that I thought she didn't know what she was talking about. I just dreaded going because I began to fear that all this overanalyzing of a comfortable life was a silly indulgence. Besides, I was always defending my involvement with McCallister, to the point that I conspired against her at all angles. So I quit. I told her I was moving to Seattle and then I stayed away from the Upper East Side as much as possible.

*

I meet Ember for the first time as she's coming out of my bathroom in one of my towels. She has a slight, angular frame, wavy dark hair, and hazel eyes that are never still. When I compliment her on her coloring, she tells me she's half Dutch, half Polynesian and pulls me over to the couch by my wrist.

"You're not from Utah, I take it," I say.

"Milwaukee," she answers. "The ghetto. I was the only white girl in my junior high. My mom's a drunk. I shared a room with my four brothers."

Ember wears her scrappy childhood as an emblem of her exoticism and toughness. I know Ford must have been smitten as soon as she told him of her origins. Although he has talked up her beauty, I am still taken with how pretty she is. She seems an altogether different species than I am. When I talk to her, it's as if she emits warmth that settles only on me.

Ford arrives just as Ember says, "Thanks for letting us stay with you. It's so cool of you."

I look at Ford but he just shrugs. I'm too tired to make it a thing and Ember's enthusiasm makes a month seem not that long.

"You're welcome," I say.

Ember wraps her smooth arms around my neck. The towel falls to her waist but she doesn't seem to care. Ford mouths "thank you" to me over her shoulder.

Ember disentangles herself from me and then sees Ford in the doorway. I leave them to their groping reunion.

chapter 5

Nikyla and Jezebel are in the lounge when I arrive at work. Nikyla is figuring out her week's earnings on a calculator and Jezebel is curling her eyelashes while flipping through an old *Cosmopolitan* that has been on the coffee table since I first came in to apply.

"Men are like Slinkies," Jezebel says. "It's fun to watch them fall down."

Nikyla smiles and shakes her head. "You'll get tired of all the running around one day when you find the right one. Hey, Roxanne."

"Hi, girls," I say.

Kendra is talking to a client on the phone, purring with sex, surrounded by Doritos, Pepsi, and cotton candy, and she waves with one long French-manicured finger.

"Diamond is out at the airport Hilton," Kendra says when she hangs up, gathering up her snacks. "You can call her out in ten."

"Diamond? I thought she quit," I say.

"She did. But she needs to get a root canal and her husband's unemployed."

I take Kendra's warm seat, and when the phone rings, I quickly book Nikyla with an old-timer who lives out near the zoo. He may be her biggest fan. She says they catch up for a while, he tells her about his grandkids, then all she has to do is take off her bra and it gets him every time.

*

The late afternoon lull has left me sleepy. I'm making halfhearted progress on a crossword puzzle when the phone rings.

"I was thinking about a new idea for a script."

"Hi, McCallister," I say.

"It's a high school movie about a gay quarterback."

"What happened to the last one?"

"It sucks. I can't finish it. Nothing's working."

"I've heard this before."

"Hey Jane?" he asks.

I hear the telltale Jaguar-door slam of Mohammed.

"Got to go. The boss has arrived."

Mohammed has a four-pack of toilet paper in one hand and a bouquet of pink carnations in the other.

"For me?" I ask. "You shouldn't have."

"We have to make things more nice around here. I was thinking about some classical music. Perhaps Chopin." Mohammed rummages around in the back for something to put the flowers in. "We are a professional establishment," he says, returning with a cloudy glass vase and handing it and the flowers to me.

"Next time," I say, "maybe not pink and not carnations." I fill the vase in the grungy bathroom sink.

"They were on special at Albertsons. A beggar cannot be a chooser."

"Why don't you bring over one of your rugs? That would spice things up in here," I say.

"A rug here? Those are works of art," he says, offended, rearranging the carnations. He opens the safe and separates the different credit card slips. "Send that new one out tonight."

"Okay. I'll send her to that guy who wants them to bark but doesn't make them do much else."

"I don't want to hear about it," he says, holding his hands to his ears. "I'm not interested in those things. Why don't you make yourself useful and clean up the bathroom while the phone isn't ringing? I pay you good money."

"Now that is definitely not in my job description," I say, going back to the crossword puzzle. "And you don't pay me that much. The rest comes from the girls."

Utah is cheap, but I'm still surprised at how easily I have adjusted to living on a fraction of what I used to make. My dad would be aghast that I no longer have a 401(k) or health insurance and that I actually have to punch in on an old-fashioned time clock.

Mohammed looks up to the ceiling and mutters an unintelligible plea. He straightens the old magazines on his way out the door without even a hello to Diamond, who brushes past him to the couch.

Diamond is twenty-one, petite but with D-cup breast implants, dark bobbed hair, and sullen brown eyes she lines in black. She got married a couple months ago and left escorting with a ceremonious salute. I was rooting for her. She got sporadic work as a fitness model, posing in a bikini next to exercise equipment in the back-page ads of muscle magazines, but the income hasn't been much.

"Hey," she says to me.

"Hey," I say, trying to sound chipper, "nice to see you."

She looks at me with an accusing glance then clicks on the TV. "Yeah, sure," she says. She turns to *Montel* and lights a cigarette. "Is Nikyla on a date? I was supposed to meet her here."

"Yeah. I sent her out again. She's with 'Randy Johnson' at the Marriott."

"That lucky bitch," she says. "I wonder what he'll buy her. Last time he took me to Victoria's Secret and got me this sexy little nightie. I wore it on my wedding night."

"How's married life?" I ask, wanting to sound cheerful.

"It's okay. It was good at first but we fight a lot." Diamond dials one of the numbers etched on the lounge phone and orders a small pepperoni pizza. "How about you, Roxanne? Ever been married?"

"Not me."

"Boyfriend?"

"No. Not since moving here."

"I can't believe you left New York for this," she says, less wistful than disgusted.

"I needed a change," I say.

Diamond gives a "whatever" shrug and turns back to the TV.

I don't tell her that I left because I had started fantasizing about my own funeral. It was almost the same thing as imagining my wedding—all the people from different stages of my life in one place, all the focus on me. Old boyfriends thinking about what might have been. McCallister in the front row. It's not that I actively wanted to kill myself but I did like that view from above.

I started with small things like giving up vitamins and vegetables, smoking alone, switching to nonlight cigarettes, not washing my hands after the subway, forgoing my seat belt and driving fast, making out with someone in a bar who had strep throat. But soon I had amassed a lethal dose of Valium. I found it calming that the option was there, that death was a possibility. I walked around late at night by myself downtown through the empty, fishy streets of Chinatown and across the Brooklyn Bridge. I avoided the dwindling, few friends who I hadn't yet shaken loose. I felt invisible, on the periphery of existence, heading toward negligible. On my bathroom mirror I taped a fortune that read, "You can always find a way out."

But when I heard that a friend from college had hung

himself in an airport bathroom stall, the vertiginous wave I felt made me flush the drugs. I wanted to be free of the mess in which I found myself but not with such finality. I wanted to be someone who would notice the color of clouds or the tang of a Fuji apple—even if I never had before. I wanted to feel things differently.

Three days later, I drove west.

*

Megan, the newest convert, arrives in tears, her body hidden under a tentlike teal blue chenille sweater. She has just come from her meeting with Detective Logan and she holds the telltale light yellow pamphlet: "Please consider your alternatives. A choice away from violence. A move away from danger. A step away from injustice. An option not to be abused. A choice toward respect. The choice is yours." I had to meet with Logan too when I applied for my license and I liked him for his rolled-up shirtsleeves and get-to-work demeanor. He'd seen it all, he told me, and this was not a business for anyone's sister, daughter, or mother to be in. He said he goes out of his way to steer girls away from escorting and bust girls and agencies whenever possible for even the tiniest infractions. Like Mohammed's, Logan's interest in the sex business didn't seem to be prurient in the least. If anything, he was paternal and I appreciated him not invoking religious doctrine in his diatribe. Although he knew he had not dissuaded me from taking the job, he was glad I was sticking to the phones and I think he believed, when he was through with me, that I'd been enlisted as a conspirator. I keep his card in my wallet.

Though rattled by her session at the police station, Megan is resolved to do what she set out to do. She swipes at her eyes with the back of her hand, and it's as if she's won a victory for a cause, for the betterment of the little guy. Evil police. Good escorts. Mohammed would be proud.

"You made it," I say to her.

"He's such a jerk," she says. "Logan acts like I could just go out and get another job or something, like I haven't tried. It's not that easy. I was a receptionist at a construction company down in Sandy but then I got laid off and then Eric left and took everything. Even my microwave."

"So what do you think about tonight?" I ask. "In addition to the normal split, twenty of your take goes back to the house until the license is paid off. I assume you want to get started as soon as possible."

Megan sits up tall to stretch out the flabby bulge of her stomach. Her eyes are glassy with alarm. Only now does it seem to hit her that she will have to get naked in front of men. There is nothing left to take care of, no more stalling. She looks to me for an answer to a question she hasn't asked. Her tongue darts to her overlapping front teeth as if for reassurance.

"I think you'll do just fine. It won't be as big a deal as you think," I say. "It'll feel good to start making some money." My pep talk sounds flat but it's enough.

"Yeah. Okay," she says.

"It will get easier," I say. "Like with anything. I'll start you off with a regular so you'll know what to expect. What's your name going to be?"

"I was thinking 'Pamela.' Like Pamela Anderson," Megan laughs. "I'll try to pretend I look like her."

"That's the spirit," I say. "We'll call you tonight if we can get you out. Seven-to-three shift. Make sure if you wear a skirt to wear pantyhose. Mohammed is pretty strict about it. Besides, it's cold out there."

"Okay," she says. "I'm ready."

Two phone lines ring at once. Megan, now Pamela, stands and hovers for a moment before turning to go. She already walks a little differently, I think, with her shoulders back, shaking her hair for effect.

When Ember calls, sounding out of breath and giddy, I immediately get caught up in the whirl of her energy.

"I heard about this place down on State Street where it hasn't changed since the seventies," she says. "The Tiki Lounge. It's super old-school. You can get drinks in bright colors with umbrellas."

"I've passed that place, I think," I say.

"So? Do you want to go?"

"Tonight?"

"Yeah, with me. Come on, it'll be fun."

chapter 6

Driving south on State Street from downtown Salt Lake, seediness and sprawl take root as the LDS temple shrinks in the rearview mirror. There is a throwback quality to the used-car dealerships, the stand-alone Sears, and the fast-food restaurants—including the country's first Kentucky Fried Chicken franchise, with its script, light-bulbed sign. After Beehive Bail Bonds, South State Street turns into a no-man's land of decay. In the gelid high desert twilight, it glows in dirty orange and yellow.

Ford, Ralf, Ember, and I are in the beat-up Saab Ember inherited from an old boyfriend, and as we take in the view of our adopted city, we manically chew gum, tap our feet, and chatter at each other. We blow our cigarette smoke out the car windows into the cold, late-fall darkness. Ember supplies the cocaine, which I took with remarkably little pause. I still feel let down that it isn't just the two of us for the outing, but the drugs help.

"Hey, have any of you ever been arrested?" Ember

asks as she gnaws her thumbnail. She pulls the car around a slow-moving pickup and speeds up.

"I got a minor in possession but I guess that doesn't really count," Ford says.

"I was caught shoplifting once," I say to the car. "When I was fourteen." Although I have always been deeply embarrassed by this, Ember makes me proud to offer it up.

That winter Saturday when I was fourteen, I took a bus to a local ski area and skied all day by myself, working on my form, taking riskier hills, skiing better than I ever had. I was so proud of myself, so excited to tell my dad. When I got home, I found him in his den, Scotch in hand, watching the news. I ran in and announced that I hadn't fallen all day.

"You must not have been trying that hard," he said.

Without a word, I left. I was so angry I went to the mall and stole a lip gloss and a pack of gum. Then, emboldened, I walked into a department store and slipped a watch into my bag. Just as I stepped out the door, a security guard grabbed my arm. When my dad came to get me at the station—the police let me go with a warning about juvenile hall—I couldn't look at him. He drove me home and to this day has never mentioned it.

"I wouldn't tell the store people who I was," I say, "so they had the police come and take me to the station. And then I cracked."

Ember smiles at me in the rearview mirror.

"Jane. I never knew," Ford says, turning around to

look at me.

Next to me, Ralf is moving to the beat of a silent song. Ember reaches back and hits his knee, and he shakes his head "no" while he continues with the rhythm.

"I have a felony record," Ember says. "In Wisconsin. I was pulled over and the cop made me stand outside in the snow on the side of the road and do those drunk-driving tests. It was so cold and he was pervy, so when he walked back to his cruiser, I packed a snowball and hurled it at him. It beaned him in the back of the head and knocked his hat off. He pulled his gun," Ember says. She sniffs and zooms through the yellow light.

"Wow," I say.

"That's pretty impressive," Ralf says to me.

Her defiance is dizzying. Now I know Ford is in love.

"Hey, you guys," I say, with newfound gameness. "I have an idea. Let's keep driving. There's a strip club where I'm supposed to pass out some cards for work. It'll be fun."

Ember laughs and honks her horn in a short-long-short succession.

"A man goes into a doctor's office," Ralf says, apropos of nothing, "and the whole left side of his body is gone. He says, 'What's my prognosis, Doc?' and the doctor answers, 'You're all right.'"

Ford laughs all the way to American Bush.

The club is a squat, shiny black building; the neon pink cat on the sign winks on and off. Inside, the air-conditioning is on despite the season, and the smell is a combination of cigars, a smoke machine, and orange-blossom perfume. It's still early in the night so there's a booth free right up near the stage and we slide in. I look up at a topless woman whose implants bulge out at the sides as she dances in high patent leather pumps. Ralf's eye twitches at the sight of her spherical breasts. Ford sees only Ember, who waves a dollar bill at the dancer above us.

"What do we have to do here again?" Ember asks. "Recruit?"

"Hand out some cards. Tell them they can make more money in the entertainment field," I say, handing a small stack of wrinkled mauve Premier business cards to her.

Ralf turns from the breasts to me, his mouth open as if asking a question.

"You don't have to talk to anyone," I say to him, "You're off the hook."

He relaxes in a slump in the booth and turns to the college basketball on one of the many TVs perched above the bar.

The dancer, a young Asian woman with waist-length ebony hair is now on the floor. She spreads her legs in our direction and pulls over her G-string, her pubic hair shaved close in a narrow strip, and I think that escorting may be better than this after all, since only one other person shares an escort's humiliation.

"So maybe I should do this escorting thing," Ember says. "It must pay pretty decently. It doesn't seem that hard." Her nose is red and running and her hands dance on the table in staccato as she talks. She looks from me to Ford and back. "Well?"

Ford keeps his eyes on Ember.

"Maybe you could look a while longer for something else," he says.

I feel for him. Despite his liberal espousals, Ford has never been that much of a free-liver.

"Maybe I could," she says.

"You can come visit me at the office," I say, "and see if it still seems interesting. I'll introduce you to Mohammed."

I can't look at Ford.

"Cool," she says.

She and Ford are in a silent standoff until he melts and touches her forehead with his. Then she's off and running with the Premier cards in hand and the buzz of an adventure. Ford watches her with softness and awe.

"You've got yourself quite a firecracker," I say.

He squints at me over his beer and drains the bottle.

"Yeah," he says, and he lets it go at that.

Ember seems to befriend everyone in the club, bartenders, dancers, and customers. I hear her laugh from some dark corner and watch her dance to the music blaring from the stage. It's smoky and dark, and above us onstage three women jiggle around with half-interested expressions, spinning around the smudged, shiny poles.

There is a dull, tight thread of irritation in my head leftover from the drugs. Although I have done cocaine before, once at a New Year's Eve party in New York a couple years ago, it isn't something I consider a casual indulgence, a mere lark. But tonight with Ember I dove right in. She went ahead and cut four lines without even giving us an option, because she'd just assumed we were with her. I liked that feeling, and going along seemed natural and fun and daring.

I stuff a dollar in a brunette's G-string and turn back to Ralf. We sit close in the booth. I don't find him particularly attractive but I consider what it would be like to kiss him. It seems uncomplicated, a healthy distraction. He says he will only marry someone who is Mormon. He brushes a hair from my face as I tell him something about what it was like to be a copywriter, how meaningless words became.

"That's so interesting," Ralf says. "I've never known a copywriter before."

I don't know what I used to do all day, hour upon hour, year after year, looking at words on a screen. I remember it as if my eyes were at half-mast.

Ford smiles at us, and then casts a worrying look into the haze after Ember.

"Tell me something about Mormonism," I say to Ralf.

"Okay," he says brightly. "Mormon was a guy. He was the leading Nephite general. He had a son named Moroni, and Moroni hid a set of golden plates in a hillside. Fifteen centuries later, the plates were revealed to Joseph Smith. That's the simple version."

"'Plates' as in dinner plates?" I ask.

"More like tablets," he says. "If you believe that hocus-pocus." He laughs and touches his bandaged chin. "Moroni is the gold angel on top of the temple."

"Good to know," I say.

Ember swoops back to the table and knocks over the last bit of my drink.

"Whew," she says, breathless. "I gave out the cards to four dancers I met. I think they're in. I said I was a talent scout."

"Thanks," I say. "Mohammed will be so pleased. You'll get twenty-five dollars for each convert."

"Including me?" she asks with a raised eyebrow.

Ember lays her head against Ford's shoulder and nuzzles his neck. He is rigid for a half second before kissing her head. Her face has a dewy glow. She catches me staring at her and leans over to kiss me on the cheek.

"Thanks for letting us stay with you, Jane," she says. "It seems like I've known you for eons."

"Hey, what about me?" Ralf asks.

Ember takes his face in her hands and kisses him on the lips. Ford smiles but I know the kiss gets him, because it gets me too.

By the time we stumble into the car it is past two. Ralf falls asleep with his head in my lap and Ember passes out in the passenger seat. Ford drives and talks quietly to me in the darkened rearview mirror.

"It's not like it seems, you know," he says.

"I don't know how it seems," I say. "And it doesn't really matter what I think about it, does it?"

Ford shrugs.

"There's something pretty compelling about always trying to catch up," I say. "Chasing that feeling of what it's like when the person picks you. I understand it, Ford, believe me."

"Sometimes I wish I didn't," he says.

I reach over and touch his head.

We don't bother taking Ralf home. The four of us go back to my apartment in the quiet Avenues, take off our shoes, and fall in a heavy, tangled mass into my bed, nestling like a litter of blind and sleepy kittens.

*

"Hello, beautiful."

"Hi, Scott."

"You sound like you might be under the weather."

"No, just a little tired," I say and yawn.

"Not too tired for me, I hope."

"Of course not."

"Great. I'll be there in a half hour."

"Hah," I say, "Nice try, baby."

"Maybe I'll drop by one day and you won't even know it's me."

"Come on now," I say, "None of that." My stomach catches. "I don't suppose you'd like to see a lady?"

With Diamond on a date, I scan the dismal list of two:

S&M Samantha with the sour disposition and the new girl, Pamela, who I found huddled and crying in the tanning closet after her first date. I don't have the heart to be the one to send her out again.

"No," he says, "not really a chance of that."

"I should get going," I say.

"You shouldn't," he says, "but I'll let you."

Just as I hang up I jump at the sound of Ember's voice.

"That sounded cozy," she says.

"Jesus. Where'd you come from?"

"Door was open. Who was that, anyway?"

"Just a caller," I say as I get up and check the lock on the door.

Ember walks over to my desk in Ford's old Irish sweater looking fresh and rested; her hair as lustrous as an oiled pelt, and her face, shiny clean. I sit back down and my head feels like a large wedge of clay propped up on my neck.

"I bet you don't talk to all the callers that way," she says. She starts to braid a section of my hair.

"Did you sleep all right?" I ask.

"Yeah. That was fun last night."

"Ford working?"

"He left before I got up. So are you going to hook me up?" she asks.

"You want to do this, just like that?" I ask.

"Why not?" she asks.

Ember gathers my hair into her hands and lets it fall on my back. I feel like I could sleep for a week. When I answer the phone, she listens with a bemused smile.

"Mohammed'll loan you the money in a second," I say to her after I hang up. "He'll think he's won the jackpot."

She hugs me from behind and reads Scott's information sheet over my shoulder.

"Maybe you could send me to that guy, the one you were talking to. He sounds like fun."

Ember spins my chair around and with a school-yard giggle, flashes me her small, perfect breasts.

"Yeah, maybe," I say, feeling a bit territorial about Scott.

Mohammed charges in and with barely an introduction, whisks Ember back into his office. A few minutes later, her laugh breaks through the afternoon dead air. I am flummoxed by the idea of her being able to jump right in, but I can't tell if it's out of envy for her guts or her beauty or her blitheness.

I'm glad when McCallister calls, because he's after something that he can get only from me.

"Jane."

"Hi."

"Do you think the gay quarterback screenplay should be a comedy or a drama?"

"Comedy."

"You're sounding particularly dour today."

"Late night." I know he is curious but I won't expound.

"Really? I was asleep at nine."

"Do you always have to use your cell phone?" I ask. "I feel like I have to yell."

"The cell phone is probably best in this situation. Besides, I can hear you just fine."

"Because I'm yelling."

"I have a question for you, Jane. Did we used to talk when we went out to dinner? I mean have stuff to talk about? Or were there long stretches of silence?"

"You talked," I say.

"Funny," he says. "It's not like it feels awkward or anything, the not talking. I just wondered."

"Every relationship is different, McCallister."

"So it is," he says.

"Got to go," I say.

Ember and Mohammed emerge with jovial smiles.

"Write out the checks," Mohammed says to me. "Let's get her out there!" He has the ebullient face of a born-again evangelist. I can't imagine what Ember gave him as collateral. He rubs his hands together and practically skips out the door.

"So what does Ford think of all this?" I ask.

"My sweet Ford," she says. "Why should he care? I'm still going home to him." From her backpack she pulls the baggie of white powder, significantly depleted from last night.

"Meet me in the bathroom?"

I hesitate but then I follow her.

Diamond buzzes as we're wiping our noses. I get the door.

"That fucker," she says as she throws herself on the couch.

I try to pinpoint her date in my racing head.

"He thinks because he's seen me before he gets privileges."

Dale, the school principal, from Bountiful.

"He got all grabby and ripped my shirt before I could get it off. Kept pushing my head down. As if."

"Where was his wife this time?" I ask.

"Some sort of ward-meeting thing. I don't know how he always gets out of church activities."

"Hey," Ember says, walking into the lounge.

"Hey," Diamond says. "Are you new?"

"Yep. I'm sure I'll see you around."

Ember smiles and waves to me on her way out.

"She's pretty," Diamond says.

"So are you," I say.

She laughs and brings the money over to the desk.

"Are you okay?" I ask. "Did he get rough or anything?"

"Whatever. I'm fine."

"How's the tooth?" I ask, to remind her that I know she's escorting again only because of that.

"It hurts like shit," she says. She smiles and tosses me a twenty-dollar bill.

*

When I get home, Ralf is sitting on my doorstep in a flannel shirt and paint-spotted jeans. His wet hair is combed back and he shivers, holding his hands under his arms.

"Where's your coat?"

"I left it in Ford's truck," he says. "I was hoping he'd be here."

"Come on in," I say. "I'll make you some tea."

He sticks his head through the door before stepping inside.

"Where is everybody?" he asks.

"I was going to ask you the same thing. Ember came in to work today."

Ralf nods and takes a seat at the kitchen table. The light is bright and sharp and it makes us shy. Through the window the crepuscular sky deepens to indigo.

"So how come they're called Latter-day Saints?" I ask.

"Because after the apocalypse, we'll be left to frolic," he says.

"Peppermint or Almond Sunset?"

"Almond Sunset," he says with a bashful smile.

I set a steaming mug in front of him and press Play on my answering machine.

"Hi honey. Well now that we got through Thanksgiving, it's time to think about Christmas. Let us know when you're coming home. Your sister has requested roast beef for Christmas dinner. You know your father and I don't care. Whatever you girls want."

I press Delete. Ralf smiles.

"Hey, are you there? Pick up. I have to ask you something. Hello? Okay. Talk to you later."

"Who's that?" Ralf asks.

"McCallister. He's in New York."

Ralf looks at me with a curious grin and drinks his tea. He seems to be without guile or pretense, which strikes me at this moment as being as appealing as fresh snow.

"You are a mysterious woman, Jane," he says finally.

I laugh. "Hardly," I say.

We move into the living room to watch TV—an old episode of *M*A*S*H*—and sit side by side on the couch, close, content, and warmed by the tea.

"Hey, feel that?" he asks.

"Yeah," I say and smile.

"Wow. I didn't know you could feel the train from way out here."

chapter 7

Ember has taken the name Shena, fittingly exotic, and she prepares for her first call out. She has tied her hair in a loose knot—no doubt for the drama of letting it down later—and looks in my closet for a sweater, opting for a snug black turtleneck.

"It's like I'm getting ready for the Oscars," she says as she smudges black eyeliner on her lids. "Sort of."

I sit on the bed and watch like an envious little sister.

"I hope you get sent to someone decent," I say.

"I'm not worried," she says as she coats her already dark lashes with mascara.

In the other room, Ford drinks beer and reads the *Deseret News*.

"Listen to what the Mormon president says," Ford calls to us. "'Our whole objective is to make bad men good and good men better, to improve people, to give them an understanding of their godly inheritance and of what they may become.' The nerve," he says.

"What do you have against improvement?" I ask,

walking out into the living room.

"I'll do it by my own rules, thank you."

"Just because it's not right for you," Ember calls back, "doesn't make it wrong."

"Good God," he says. "Since when did the two of you convert?"

When Ember appears in the doorway, Ford winces, recoiling into his body. She is stunning. The energy crackles silently between the three of us.

He turns away and drains his beer. She goes into the kitchen and cuts lines of cocaine on the kitchen counter. She snorts two of them and I have one. Ford won't join us.

The phone rings as if on cue and a flinch passes across Ember's face. She quickly hides it with a smile when she sees me watching. I asked the phone girls to be easy on her, but the name of the date is no one I know.

Ember kisses Ford's head, then bites the back of his neck until he scrunches his shoulders and succumbs, and they giggle and kiss. I volunteered to be Ember's driver, to make the process less solitary and severe, so I wait for them to disentangle themselves, jangling my keys.

"Don't wait up," she finally says to Ford, striking a screen siren's pose.

Seeing Ford's distress, I almost shift sides but Ember pulls my hand with all the strength of her wiry, electric body, and I trip after her to the car.

"Are you freaked out?" I ask, once we've closed the doors.

I can see my breath in the front seat. Ember tunes the radio to hip-hop.

"No way. It's an adventure."

The drug flips a hyperawareness switch in my head and I am vicariously expectant for whatever the evening holds. Ember dances in her seat like she is getting pumped up for a boxing match.

"Be good," I say. "It's harder than you think to tell who's a cop."

She smiles as we drive by the Christmas lights display in Temple Square, and I smile at good old Moroni on top. Below him, each tree shimmers with tiny lights setting off the spotlighted granite spires of the temple.

"That's why the streets are so wide here," I say, pointing to the church, "so the oxcarts carrying the granite to build the steeples could turn around."

"Did Ralf tell you that?"

I laugh.

"It really does look like Disneyland," she says.

One of the horse-drawn tour carriages pulls out into our lane and I slam on the brakes, acutely sensitive to keeping everything in control in my current state.

"We should do that some time before Christmas," Ember says, pointing to the carriage. "Just you and me. It'll be sad and fun."

"And cold," I say.

"Maybe when it gets all snowy."

"Yeah," I say, "okay."

Little America is a sprawling hotel complex that gives off an air of middle-class suburbia despite its location downtown. There are small patches of lawn around the faux colonial buildings. Mormons like to stay here when they come to pay tribute to the founding fathers. We send a lot of girls here.

After a few turns around the parking lot, we find number 206, one of the apartmentlike low brick units far from the cheery main reception. Ember turns off the radio.

"My lipstick okay?" she asks, rubbing her nose.

I nod.

"Let's get this party started," she says as she opens the door.

In the shadowy light, Ember is small, fluttery, and fast, like an erratic bird heading straight for a window it can't see. Up the outside stairs, she makes her way along the corridor and stops in front of 206. Without hesitation, she thrusts her hip out and knocks with rapid-fire certainty.

When she slips inside the room, I ungrip the steering wheel. I pick at my dry cuticles and look to the hotel room door again and again. In a messy pile down by her floor mat are the papers Ember has amassed in the process of officially becoming an escort. On the top, with a footprint bisecting it, is the city ordinance list.

ORDINANCE 5.61.040 DEFINITIONS
"Escort" means any person who, for pecuniary compensation, dates, socializes, visits, consorts

with or accompanies or offers to date, consort,
socialize, visit, or accompany another or others to
or about social affairs, entertainment, or places of
amusement, or within any place or public or private resort or any business or commercial establishment or any private quarters.

ORDINANCE 5.61.085A
A licensed outcall employee may appear in a state
of nudity before a customer or patron providing
a written contract for such appearance was
entered into between the customer or patron and
the employee and signed at least twenty-four
hours before the scheduled nude appearance.

Even Mohammed is willing to let us slide on the
second one. His lawyer has advised us that stapling a back-
dated "Nudity Notice" to a client sheet will do the job.

Ember has drawn daisies and irises down the margin
of Mohammed's "Escort Training Manuel."

6. You should dress appropriately to maximize your
income. It is suggested that if you smoke, you should
wash your hands and chew gum before the appointment. Remember, too, that clients may not appreciate
foul language.

I click off the overhead light; I'm on edge about Ember and by extension uncertain about what I am doing. A middle-aged man in a Russian fur hat stops on the sidewalk in front of my windshield. Although it is dark and I am still, he notices my eyes reflecting the lamplight. We hold a gaze and something of a leer jags at one corner of his mouth until his plump wife scampers up beside him and they walk off toward the dining room.

"Fuck you," I say, once he's safely gone. My voice sounds foreign and meek in the close car.

I put the radio on continual scan and let the song snippets and half-words of ads and DJs alight on my brain and then dissipate. With a half hour to go I leave the toasty haven of the car for the pay phone at the end of the lot.

"Hello?"

"Did I tell you Ford was staying with me?"

McCallister has always been a little jealous of Ford—the way he stepped outside urban life to forge his own sort of macho path, his hairline, the fact that he knew me first. He's afraid I think Ford is cooler than he is.

"Really. For how long?"

"For a few more weeks. His girlfriend is here too," I can feel his relief at the mention of her. "I'm waiting for her in a hotel parking lot. She's on her first escort date."

"Jesus," McCallister says. "Is it one of those fleabag places?"

"No. It's mostly Mormon."

"They must have beds as wide as football fields."

"Funny," I say.

"Maria's meeting me in a couple of minutes. Dinner with her parents."

"Lucky you," I say.

"What did you want, anyway?" he asks. "You never call me."

"I don't know. I was bored, I guess. Did you know it's illegal for an escort to spank a client if he is in his underwear, but if he's nude, it's legal?"

I hear a woman's voice.

"Well, thanks for calling," McCallister says in a business tone.

I sigh and call him an asshole, but only after I've hung up.

Back inside the car, I turn the heat to high, lean my seat back and feel my skin warm down to my toes. I had told myself that my contact with McCallister wasn't holding me back as long as I was never the one who called. In my disappointment with my weakness, I tear at a hangnail with my teeth until I taste blood.

From the back window of the car, the moon hangs large and yellow. I try to believe that I am floating in the present but my mind tumbles and spins, bumping up against the fear of what I am supposed to do next. I have been in Utah for a half year. I no longer have the excuse that I'm still getting settled. The little money I came with is gone. Part of me wants to be in room 206 with Ember. Surely there wouldn't be much else to think about than the task at hand.

*

"It wasn't that big a deal," Ember says. "Really. I don't get what all the fuss is about. I just made a hundred dollars for an hour."

A piece of Ember's hair is caught on her lip and she swats it away as if it were a dogged fly. She punches in the lighter on the dashboard and digs around her purse.

"Here," I say, handing her a cigarette.

"Thanks," she says. She lights it, closes her eyes, and takes a deep drag. "Much better."

I go first to McDonald's to get Ember a caramel sundae, then on to Premier, where I wait in the car while she settles up. I'm jittery. I smoke without really wanting to. I tune the radio to *Car Talk* on NPR; I yearn for such a simple sequence of cause, effect, solution.

Ember is back a minute later with an impishness restored to her smile.

"So, Jane," she says, counting out her money.

"Yeah?"

"What do you want to know?"

I turn the car out of the alley onto Second South.

"Tell me everything," I say.

I drive west out of downtown, over the train tracks, and out past the airport where the lights become sparse along the south edge of the Great Salt Lake. We can smell it even in the cold with the windows up, even though we can't see it. The snow-topped Wasatch Mountains to the east have a lunar glow. I turn in at Saltair; its washed-out, primary-colored onion domes are dream shapes against the clear night sky. This used to be a place where Mormons would come for family fun, "the Coney Island of the West." Thousands danced in the pavilion. There was even a roller coaster. Now it houses a gift shop selling saltwater taffy and salt licks in the shape of Utah, and outdated arcade games, and occasionally it hosts the concert of a has-been performer. But in winter it's sealed up, its windows covered with padlocked boards. I park with the headlights on the choppy lake water that laps at the salt-encrusted rocky shore. The forceful wind gently rocks the car. I turn off the engine and wait for Ember to talk.

"He had a vague resemblance to Tom Hanks," Ember says. "If Tom Hanks were short and puffy and bald on the top. He shook my hand and said, 'Shena?' I laughed when he said it, and then I felt bad because he blushed."

I have the anticipatory pang in my stomach, like the moment after ingesting a drug or stepping into a pair of expensive shoes. Ember leans her seat back and puts her feet against the glove compartment.

"He had a fan of twenties already on the table next to the bed, which he knew to give me at the beginning. It's hard to tell if he calls escorts a lot. He wasn't relaxed but he wasn't unfamiliar with it all, if that makes any sense. 'So Tony,' I said, 'why don't you make yourself comfortable?' Like they say in the movies. He sat on the edge of the bed, took off his shoes, then looked at me to make the next move."

"Did you talk to him?"

"I asked him things like 'Are you from Salt Lake?' and he said no but I could tell he was lying. Probably married. 'What do you do?' Software salesman. He wasn't exactly effusive but he was totally polite. He asked my permission for everything. I made all my actions very slow and deliberate to eat up as much time as possible. Scarf unwrapped. Coat off. I sat next to him on the bed and leaned over him to find an R&B station on the clock radio. I helped him unbutton his shirt. He liked that."

"Were all the lights on?"

"At that point I made a production out of slow dancing around the room, letting my hair down, turning off some of the lights, shaking my ass for him, taking off my shoes, putting my foot up on the table to take off my stockings one leg at a time. I felt his eyes on me always but I liked it. It wasn't that icky. He seemed harmless."

"Was he naked yet?"

"No. Down to boxers. But not touching himself or anything. He asked me how old I was, how long I'd been an escort."

"What'd you say?"

"Twenty-three. One week."

"He must have been psyched."

"He pulled back the bedspread and leaned against the pillows. I made a lot of eye contact. After I pulled my shirt over my head I tossed it at him. I tried to make two minutes go by before the skirt came off but time is so damn slow when you want it to go fast."

"What did you do when commercials came on the radio?"

"I asked him what he wanted me to do."

"And?"

"'Just keep doing what you're doing, baby' he said, 'Show me your ass.' He said that a lot. So I was down to bra and undies and I danced like the girls did at American Bush. Lots of leaning over in various directions, grinding, moving my hands all over. Then he asked if I was cold, which I was, so he said I should join him on the bed."

"Weren't you scared?"

"I mean, yeah, kind of. I gave him sort of a lap dance—he had the covers pulled up—and let him touch me some. He was gentle. His hands were warm and smooth."

"Bra on or off?"

"On. But I let him take it off."

Ember is making lines of white powder on a Johnny Cash CD case.

"I think the key is going to be pity," she says. "I felt sorry for this guy."

"Did you kiss him?"

"Yeah, but no tongue. He smelled like Old Spice. Like my dad. We rolled around the bed, both with underwear on."

"Did he try stuff?"

"Not really. He rubbed his boner against my leg but

that was okay. He licked my boobs. He kept saying, 'Shena, you're so pretty.' But he didn't ask for a blow job or sex or anything."

"How much time was left?"

"There were about five minutes before the call so I pulled away and got fully naked. I lay on my back and showed him my cootch. He jacked off, then he whimpered like a little boy."

There is so much distance in Ember's retelling, I feel like I'm watching from the back row of the balcony section. I can't get at it, whatever it is.

She snorts cocaine with one of her newly acquired bills.

"Wow, I'm a cliché," she says. She laughs as she wipes the powder from her nostril.

"So then what?" I ask.

"Kendra called. He didn't want to extend. I got dressed, he thanked me, kissed me on the cheek, and gave me fifty bucks extra."

Headlights, one of them dim, approach in the rearview. A beat-up van drives into the parking lot, but when it sees our car, it drives back out onto the frontage road.

"Maybe we should go see what Ford is up to," Ember says.

"What are you going to tell him?"

"Just about nothing," she says.

On the way to town, I stop at AM/PM for more cigarettes and then the drive-through at Arctic Circle.

"Do you have any siblings?" Ember asks, between fries.

"A sister. She's older. We're not that close. She's a real estate agent and lives outside of Chicago with her lawyer husband. She thinks I'm having some sort of third life crisis. Which I may well be."

By the time I was ten and my sister was fifteen, she had moved on from me, and my clamoring for her attention only made her retreat more. She has always yearned for structure—even as a child she made a diagram of her wedding—and she planned her life accordingly. I, on the other hand, wanted something or someone to lead me in the other direction. I would say we are amicably estranged, confused by each other but not willing to make the effort to get past it. I called her when McCallister and I broke up, but she said she never could understand why I had liked him in the first place.

"One of my brothers is in jail for drugs," Ember says. "One's in the army in Texas. One is a steamfitter in Milwaukee. He's the most normal. And one's dead. He died last year when this chick hit him with a brick."

"I'm sorry," I say.

"Don't be. He was an asshole. He tried to rape me when I was twelve."

Ember has her feet up on the glove compartment again; her skirt pushed up like a tomboy's, her hair in a high ponytail, and her hamburger resting on her knees.

She looks ten years younger than she did before her date.

"I miss the idea of my brothers," she says. "But I don't really miss them as people."

I take the long way home, up along the ridge of the Avenues with a perfect view of the graph of lights in the valley and the fantastically lit temple glowing at its heart. Whatever one thinks of Mormon ideology, the way they took control of this place, bent it to their will, and forced unforgiving land to make sense is admirable.

"Hey look," Ember says, pointing up to a streetlight.

For the first time this season, it's begun to snow.

chapter 8

Although I wake up to a glorious white-covered morning, by the afternoon all the snow has melted in the unrelenting valley sun. As I drive to work, the last shaded patches are seeping into the ground.

Inside the office, Jezebel and Nikyla are decorating a fake Christmas tree Mohammed brought in to make the workplace more festive. Albee drags a wad of tinsel through their feet.

"I need another box," Jezebel says, after tossing a handful of tinsel on the tree without discretion. "This side is totally naked."

Nikyla carefully hangs frosted-glass ornaments in even spaces between the artificial limbs of the tree.

"Maybe if you hung the strands individually, it wouldn't end up so lopsided," Nikyla says.

Jezebel moves from the tree and hangs tinsel on Nikyla's shoulders, head, and breasts, until Nikyla gives her a playful shove.

"Come on, Rox, help us out here," Nikyla says.

But the phone is ringing so I skitter over to answer it, setting up a date for S&M Samantha with a once-a-weeker in Federal Heights, before even sitting down.

"I can't believe you pushed that whore instead of me," Jezebel says, draping her arm around Nikyla. "I'm totally broke. Albee is so fucking expensive."

"You couldn't have gone anyway," Nikyla says.

"Hey, Roxanne," Jezebel says. "You should come with us!"

"Come with you where?" I ask.

"Bachelor party. These guys coming in from L.A. out at Alta. Come on. It's the best setup."

"We'll show you what to do," Nikyla says.

"I don't think so," I say. "I'm not ready for that."

"But you're considering it?" Nikyla asks.

"I guess," I say shyly, though the thought of dancing around next to these two nubile beauties in a roomful of chanting drunken men seems scarier and more exposing than rolling around on a bed with a stranger.

"Oh come on," Jezebel says, fingering her bottom lip like a toddler, "don't be a party pooper."

Nikyla winks at me. "Another time, Rox. When you're ready."

"Thanks," I say.

But as they bustle around, painting their faces, laughing, spraying perfume, I want to be one of them. I'm jealous even though I'm not quite sure of what.

"They booked us for two hours," Nikyla says, "but since it's early I'm sure they'll want us longer."

Jezebel says, "As if they would tell two hot naked girls, 'Okay, you can go now.'"

They set off, done up like party-going teenagers, and leave me alone with the half-tinseled tree. I turn on a lamp in the lounge to save the tree from the obfuscating darkness but it's tilted and more blaringly metal and plastic in the light. The void from the girls' departure is heavy and quiet. I start hoping they forgot something and will come back for me.

When the door flies open, I jolt out of my chair but it's just Mohammed with a wreath in one hand and a bag of lights in the other.

"It's looking better in here," he says.

"Since when do Muslims celebrate Christmas?" I ask.

"Hah. I am an American," he says, shaking his fist in the air. He takes a roll of stringed lights from the bag and hands it to me. "Start at the top of the tree and work your way down. Next year maybe we'll get one of those fluffy trees that's all white."

"Flocked?"

"Flocked. Yes," he says. "That would be nice."

He sticks a cluster of plastic thumbtacks into the door and hangs the pine wreath, already dried out and starting to brown in patches.

"That new girl quit. Megan who called herself Pamela. After one lousy date. Can you believe this? I went out on a limb for her, gave her a chance, and look at the thanks I get."

"I think she was pretty traumatized. It took me twenty minutes to get her to stop crying after the date."

"What did she think she'd be doing? Dinner and a movie? That crummy bracelet of hers isn't worth anything. We have to be more careful about who we take on. I mean this."

Mohammed straightens the wreath.

"I'll be at the Saharan," he says.

He shuts the door behind him and a sprinkle of needles falls to the carpet.

*

Ford, Ember, and Ralf are drinking whiskey in the kitchen when I get home. Ember is making popcorn while the other two play chess at the table.

"One big happy family," I say.

"Jane!" Ember says. "We've missed you."

She kisses my cheek and hands me a glass. I catch what looks like envy shadow Ford's face. Ralf smiles up at me through his shaggy bangs then goes back to concentrating on the board. Ford pulls me onto his lap.

"How's the house going?" I ask.

"We put in the windows today," he says.

Finishing the house means Ford will leave in a week. I don't ask whether Ember will be going with him. It doesn't seem like she'll be going back to waitressing in

Moab anytime soon. From the way she flits around the kitchen, I can tell she's been into the drugs again. She comes over and hugs me and puts her warm cheek next to mine. I drink.

"Are you working tomorrow?" Ember asks. "I am," she says before I answer. "I hope you're on. I want you to be the one who sends me out."

"Jane," Ralf says after moving his knight, "did you know that the Mormons are so well-ordered that they have three levels of heaven? The Celestial, Terrestrial, and Telestial Kingdoms."

"So you're saying I might have a shot?" I ask.

"Even the mere-mortal nonbelievers have hope of getting into the lowest one, the Celestial Kingdom. I imagine it's not so bad," he says, downing the rest of his whiskey.

"It's heaven at least," I say.

"You'll do all right," Ralf says.

Ember plunks down a big bowl of warm popcorn on the table. We each take greedy handfuls. Ford moves his rook.

Ember situates herself on Ralf's lap as if she were a child, as if it were the most natural thing. He is surprised though clearly pleased to have been selected as her seat. The whiskey forms a thin warm layer around me.

"Okay, Jane," Ember says, biting her lip. "Let's play a game. For one minute—that's sixty *Mississippis*—I dare you to stand there and show us your boobs."

"What kind of game is that?" I ask.

Ford shifts underneath me in the chair. Ralf's mouth is open and he's trying not to smile. Ember grins and throws a popcorn kernel at me. I am torn between panic and thrill. I take the stage.

It's an odd feeling, all those eyes of anticipation on me. I'm somehow shamed even in my pre-nakedness. But I am also the one chosen and I don't want to disappoint. I feel close to powerless in that spotlight, unable to break the contract. To fulfill their expectation, I must follow through. I stand in the middle of the linoleum-floored kitchen and, without a word, lift off my sweater, then my shirt, and watch them as they watch me in my bra. Ember smiles and counts. Ralf is beatific. Ford glances at my breasts—breasts he's seen before—then looks up and holds my gaze. But the frosty air that slips through the ill-fitting windows gives me goose bumps and at once I lose my nerve.

"I can't do it," I say.

"Pussy," Ember says.

"I know it shouldn't be that big a deal. But…"

"It's all right," she says. "We still love you."

I pull my shirt back on and ball up my sweater, tossing it into the corner. Instead of Ford's lap, I opt for the floor. The stunt has left me feeling provoked.

"Ford," I say, "I have a question."

He takes a sip of his drink and crosses his arms to prepare himself.

"What do you really think about Ember being an escort?" I ask.

He drops his head briefly, resting his chin on his chest and pursing his lips. Although I know he is angry about the ambush, he keeps any evidence of it from his face. If anything, he looks a bit bewildered. He picks up a chess piece and taps it against the table.

"Interesting question," Ember says. "I'm curious to hear the answer myself."

The tone of the room has darkened but I fight the urge to lighten it. Ford has yet to utter a syllable.

"Maybe we should go to the movies," Ralf says under his breath.

"What do I think of my girlfriend being an escort," Ford says, leaning forward, only looking at me. "Well, Jane, if you must know, I'm not so comfortable with it. In fact I would rather she didn't do it. Okay? There it is."

I got what I wanted and now I want to give it back.

"Okay," I say, having lost my swagger, "okay."

Ember tries to restore some levity to the mood. "Okay, okay, okay. That's enough of that."

She springs from Ralf's lap, and with her back to us, she chops cocaine on the counter. I can't look at Ford. My face burns. Ember snorts everything without offering it to anyone else.

"Hey, you guys," Ralf says, "let's do something else. Come on."

"Let's just forget it," I say. "I'm going to go to bed." I

stand and carry glasses to the sink.

"Bed?" Ember asks, rubbing her nostrils. "I'm not the least bit tired. Come on. We're going out. I need to be at the Zephyr at midnight."

I assume this means Ember has to meet the dealer she has befriended, thus her sniffing up all of her supply. She squeezes my shoulder before turning to pull Ralf and Ford by the hands out of their seats. They wrap themselves in their coats and scarves, and Ember is the first one out the door.

"Ford," I say, grabbing his forearm, "I'm sorry. I don't know why I did that."

"I have some ideas about why," he says, "but it's okay. It should have been said long before tonight."

He puts his hand around the back of my neck and I welcome the briefest sense of rootedness. And then he's gone.

After they leave, I don't go to bed. Instead I drive farther up into the Avenues to Smith's, the bright grocery mecca that I find as consoling as my morning coffee. The wide-aisled, expansive grocery stores of Utah, where space and bounty are as limitless as the geniality of the clean-cut checkout clerks, make for ideal places to hide. The piped-in soft-rock songs are so poignant that I sometimes sing along, misty-eyed, and don't want to be anywhere else.

I stand in front of a wall of glass-fronted freezers in the interminable ice cream section. It's late and I am alone. I wonder how many other women have stood here, desperate for comfort, hoping to find solace in what they know is bad for them and ultimately unfulfilling. I pull down a carton of double-fudge brownie, take a plastic spoon from the deli counter, and start in before the mere half-mile drive home is over.

I haven't even taken off my coat when I notice white dust on the counter. I wipe my finger across the surface to consolidate the remains, then press my fingertip on the tiny mound and rub it on my gums. The drug hits surprisingly fast and sharp, and I eat the rest of the ice cream without even tasting it, without even noticing it going down, with only a vague satisfaction of indulging an urge.

I lick the sticky, chocolate edge of the sweaty carton, replace the lid, and bury it deep in the trash, under the eggshells and coffee grounds. As I crawl into bed feeling sick, I have the dark sensation of having reached a new depth of solitude.

*

The office is stuffy and quiet, a strip of afternoon sun showing dusty through a broken blind slat. I answer the phone.

"How may I help you?"

"Jane."

"McCallister."

"Do you think it's true that organization springs from anxiety?"

"Um, it's possible, I guess. This state is a pretty good example. The perfectly tidy streets and tidy patriarchies and tidy rules for living. But there's mess lurking underneath. I read that the majority of murders in Utah are husbands killing wives."

"Maybe because they have so many extras," he says.

"McCallister."

"Just a joke."

"What brings this up?"

"Maria has become obsessed with neatness. She can't make coffee if there is anything in the sink. She can't sleep if there's a sock on the floor. But I know she's just anxious about what happens when we move in together."

"Are you worried?"

"Yeah. Maybe."

And before I can get it back I say, "Good. You should be," and hang up to answer the other line.

"Hi, beautiful," Scott says.

"Hi," I say, "I'm glad it's you." And I am. The boundaries are clear.

"In that case, I have a proposal," he says.

"Would you like to see someone?" I ask weakly.

"I can't today. But tomorrow night I would. You and me. Almost like a real date."

I'm sweating through my turtleneck. I know it won't get any easier than this to jump in.

"Roxanne?"

"Okay," I say.

There is silence.

"Really?" he asks.

"Yes," I say. "Yes."

At once I feel giddy and subversive and somehow important. I can take this route, this risk. Because I dare myself. Because I can. I scribble out an escort application and schedule my health exam appointment for tomorrow.

ӿ

I still feel pretty manic when I leave work, so with my excess energy I do things that I've been meaning to for months: I go to the post office for stamps, get a new windshield wiper blade, replace the batteries in the smoke detector, caulk the bathroom sink, refill the salt shaker.

The last of the daylight is filtering through the bare walnut tree outside the kitchen window. And then I remember one more thing I've been meaning to do since I arrived in Utah. I get in the car and race the waning light, driving east to the end of the 1,300-mile Mormon Trail, where the pioneers first entered the Salt Lake Valley. I pass the cabins of Old Deseret Village, where schoolchildren come for wagon rides and "visits" from costumed Mormon historical figures, and I continue up the hill to the monument that marks Brigham Young's "This is the place" proclamation.

Outside the wind bites, and it is quiet at the mouth of the canyon. Atop a sixty-foot granite pedestal overlooking the valley is a bronze figure of Brigham Young with his giant finger outstretched, flanked by other church forefathers, a memorial of the struggle-and-triumph conceit so integral to Mormon cultural myth.

A year ago, I stood on my rickety fire escape and breathed in the dirty city air. I looked at the rusted bars under my feet and wondered—if they gave way and I fell three stories to the icy sidewalk, would I die? Would that do it?

My fingers have gone stiff in the Utah cold, but my head feels clear and clean.

Yes. Like a rosary bead I finger the word, revisit it. Yes is a moment, a mix of calm and readiness.

The lights come on as I'm staring up at the pioneers, as if someone saw me looking into the darkness. I laugh, but I look around and I am alone.

I drive toward the valley lights and home.

chapter 9

Marisa is working the phone and she is unfazed when I call and tell her that I want to be sent out. She doesn't ask why now, if I'm apprehensive, what changed my mind. She either assumed I would do it eventually or has learned to assume nothing. And I am thankful.

Apparently having patched things up from the night before, Ford and Ember went to Wendover to play black-jack. I didn't tell them what I have decided to do; I cradle the secret like a china doll. It is all mine.

I prepare myself for Marisa's call with a bath. I welcome the hottest water, willing myself to feel it against my skin as I submerge. The bathroom is dark except for some old candles I rounded up in an attempt to commemorate the night. I shave slowly and deliberately all the way up my thighs, bikini line and all, going over every inch with multiple swipes of a new razor. I exfoliate my elbows. I sit on the edge of the tub and paint my toenails poppy red. I wonder if this is how a bride in an arranged marriage feels before her wedding night. Except I still have the option of saying no. But the phone rings, and I know I won't.

"Hi." It's McCallister. "I can't believe you hung up on me. Again."

"I can't talk right now."

"Why not?"

"I'm waiting for a call."

"Why so cryptic?"

"It's a date."

"A date?"

"Yeah."

"With Ford?"

"Of course not."

"Then with whom?"

"A setup. A blind date."

"Wow. I guess I'm supposed to say good luck."

"That would be the nice thing."

"But if it works out, you'll never come back to New York. So I won't."

"Always the selfless one, aren't you, McCallister?"

"Just looking out for you."

"This conversation will have to wait," I say.

"Fine," he says, and this time it's McCallister who hangs up.

I opt for a scarlet silk dress over a new black lace bra and underwear. The silk is soft and warm against my skin. I gloss my lips and spray expensive perfume I never use, an old gift from McCallister, on each side of my neck. I feel glamorous. I sing along with the soulful, plaintive voice of Ray Charles—"I'm gonna love you, like no one's loved you, come rain or come shine"—as I check out how I look from various angles in the mirror. I turn off the lights and have a cigarette by the glow of Christmas lights dripping from the neighbors' houses, and blow smoke out the window into the frosty darkness. Toward the end of the second cigarette, Marisa calls.

"You're in luck. Scott requested you. He's at the Monaco. Room 1023. Eight o'clock. Maybe you'll get room service," she says.

"Maybe," I say. "He didn't want to do a public date?"

"You're not that lucky," she says.

I feel like there should be more business to take care of, something I'm supposed to ask. I grind out my cigarette and the ashtray tips, dumping ashes out onto the carpet.

"Shit," I say.

"Roxanne?"

"Yeah?"

"Are you okay?"

"I'm fine," I say.

"Call me when you get there."

It's a perfect, high-desert, early-winter night in Salt Lake City—cloudless and brisk with a moon just shy of full. The houses in the Avenues are warmly lit. The streets are empty. Inside my thawing car, Bob Dylan is on the classic rock station. I feel like a movie star.

I'm only about seven minutes from the Monaco so I make a few loops around Temple Square. Mormon visitors promenade around the block of Main Street that the church purchased from the city to connect the square to the palatial new conference center. Whole families hold hands. The contentment on their faces is enviable. Linked together in this holy destination, they seem wanting of nothing.

Although it's Friday night, I easily find a parking spot only a block from the hotel. I breathe deeply, exhaling through my mouth, as I once learned in a yoga class. A quick makeup check in the rearview mirror, a readjusting of my pantyhose, an Altoid, a brief thought of McCallister, gesticulating with chopsticks the night he said he didn't think we should see each other anymore, and I'm off.

The Monaco is an anomaly for Salt Lake City, an expensive boutique hotel with sharp angles and dramatic lighting and a cozy wine bar right out of TriBeCa. It's the first time I've ever been inside, and its un-Utah-ness lends it a movie-set quality. Despite the chic environment, I feel conspicuously harlotlike with my red lips and my red hem peaking out from beneath my coat, even if no one seems to notice me. I make it across the lobby without looking up, grateful to be swallowed up by an empty elevator. If it's not going to be a fake real date in public, I'm at least glad it's here and not the Econolodge or the Dream Inn out on North Temple. I press ten as I catch a glimpse of myself in the chrome ceiling of the elevator.

At the door to room 1023, my knock is wimpy and

I'm just about to knock again when I see the door is not clasped shut and a deeper version of the voice I recognize says, "Come on in."

I count to three, arrange my face in what feels like my most confident, mature, knowing, sexy look—even though I'm sweating and I have an odd urge to cross myself—and I slowly push open the door.

The softly lit room is a sea of dark browns and black. My heels sink deep into the plush carpet where I have stopped just inside the door. Scott sits near the window, his ankle crossed on his knee and his arms stretched out around the back edge of the chair. He looks like an aging ex-athlete, like a minor-league player who never got his shot at the majors. He is not far off from what I expected and this is both a relief and a letdown. His hair is, as his client sheet said, ash-blond, a little receding in front, a little too long in back. He is, if not altogether handsome, attractive in a self-assured, masculine way.

I feel excited and I feel like I might throw up. From moment to moment I feel the power shift from me to Scott, back and forth. I can't decide who's winning. I finger a button on my coat, unsure whether to proceed or to wait for further instruction. I am at once myself and someone altogether new. The curtains are pulled open and the lights of the valley shimmer like so many stars. I remember that I have to call my parents and tell them that I'm not coming home for Christmas. I think about whether Ember and Ford are gambling away money they don't have, and whether Ember will leave with Ford. I tell myself that meeting a man in a hotel room for money is just another thing to try. My stomach growls. I roll my shoulders back and smile a closed-lipped, enigmatic smile.

There is a cockiness in the way Scott tilts his head and sizes me up. For a full minute he looks at me and grins as I stand there in the entrance. I'm getting paid not to turn away.

"Hi, beautiful," he says. "It's nice to see you."

*

"Are you safe?" Marisa asks.

"Yes," I say into the phone. My face burns as I stand by the bed. Scott hasn't moved.

"Have you collected?"

"Yes."

I'm still clutching the bank-new bills. When he pulled the crisp stack from his wallet, I couldn't bring myself to count it. I stuff the money in my coat pocket.

"Okay, Roxanne, good luck. I'll call you out in fifty."

"Bye," I say, wanting to keep her on the line, wanting to run for the door, wanting to be in the front row at the movies with a large popcorn and McCallister on a rainy Saturday afternoon.

"So. Why don't you take off your coat and stay a while?"

Scott has uncrossed his legs and now leans forward with his elbows on his knees, his fingers laced between them. A nervous tightness around his mouth makes his smile stiff and unnatural.

"Okay. Sure."

In the past few minutes my confidence has seeped out. I think that the polite thing for him to do would be to help me out of my coat, but he is as still as marble. All right then. I shake my shoulders until my coat slips down my arms. I know the effect would be better if I let it fall to the floor in a romantic cascade, but I'm starting to feel like I don't owe him anything so I place it first on the bed, then reconsider and move it to a chair. I lift my hair off my neck to feel some coolness and I try to resettle the composure that I know my face has lost.

"That's better," Scott says. "What I want to know is why you put me off for so long, anyway. The chemistry was so clear on the phone."

There is a hole in his ear from an old piercing and his fingernails are bitten. I look from detail to detail for insight or distraction. Not knowing what to do next to ease the awkwardness, I fall to my knees and untie his shoes, slowly working each socked foot from his barely worn oxfords. He has dressed up for me. He blinks his baby-long lashes in a quizzical flurry, as if going for the feet was more intimate than an escort is allowed to be; too forward, too fast.

"Are you married?" I ask, rubbing the arch of his foot.

"Me? Are you kidding? Why would I be calling you all?"

"You wouldn't be the first," I say, taking the heel of his other foot in my hand. "Girlfriend?"

"Oh, that feels nice. Girlfriend? No. Not at the moment," he says, letting his head rest against the back of the chair. "We broke up a few months ago. She wanted to get married. Mormons think they're spinsters if they're not married by thirty. I don't even think I was in love."

"Have you ever been in love?" I ask.

I'm stalling. Scott now seems more like a country singer than he does an athlete. I pull off his socks just to have something to do. His feet are white and clammy but not as gross as they could be.

"Yeah, I guess. I'm not some sort of freak or anything," he says, running his fingers through the side wing of his hair.

"Of course you're not," I say.

I lean back on my hands and look at him, wondering whether he is scrutinizing me—if he sees the pimple on the top of my forehead, the freckles on my nose, the wrinkles at the corners of my eyes—or if he sees me at all. Maybe he just sees what he imagined me to be from the phone. My thoughts descend from "He is a lucky bastard" to "I hope I'm not a letdown."

"Wouldn't you be more comfortable over there?" I ask, pointing my eyes toward the bed.

Scott clears his throat and looks down for a moment as if to think it over. His smile is catlike when he looks up again. I wonder how much time has been used up but I don't dare glance at the clock.

"I just might be," he says.

I shift back on my heels and he hops up from his seat. I hold out my hand in the direction of the bed like a game show model displaying the showcase prize. He sits first with his feet on the floor but then scowls, swiveling around to lean against the headboard, crossing his legs straight out in front on the bed. I have an urge to settle in next to him and see what movies are on. Instead I push him gently forward to stuff the pillows behind his back.

"Now isn't that better," I say, attempting to embody the character of my phone voice.

"Much," he says. He crosses his arms across his chest and grins like a boy caught in a bad lie. "Show me what you got."

I am unnerved by this but I try to let it slide. He is becoming more of a type, a subset of maleness. I want to be back in command. One by one, I lift a foot behind me, arching, to slip off my shoes. Scott cocks his head like a puppy. Like Ember, I lift my leg up against the side of the table, slipping the fishnet stockings slowly down thigh and calf and pointed toe. One, and then the other. The curtains are open and in front of me is the southern sprawl of the valley, its grid of lights grounding me for a moment before I resume and toss my stockings on the floor near my shoes.

"I knew you'd have nice legs," Scott says. "Let's see them."

I arrange one leg in front of the other like a beauty pageant contestant—hoping he doesn't scrutinize my thighs—and slowly slide my dress up, the soft silk grazing my legs, until it's just below my underwear.

"So you like to hunt and play golf?" I ask, realizing how ridiculous I sound, standing there with my dress pulled up to my waist. But Scott laughs and eases the moment and I slowly take a turn on my imaginary catwalk.

"Uh huh," he says, "Now lift it higher and show me your ass."

I bite my lip and do what he asks, then bend over, making small rotations with my hips. This seems to be the right thing. Scott gives a small whistle.

"I need some help with this," I say, fiddling with the zipper in back of my dress.

I'm surprised at my willingness to lose my dress without even needing a nudge, but it seems like the obvious next motion in the sequence. As I sit gingerly on the edge of the bed, Scott unzips me. His large damp palms push the straps of the dress down over my shoulders with a certainty that makes me anxious and I'm glad to be turned away from him. His hands travel over my back and I can only think "hot" and then I think for a second, "not clean," and when I eye the clock, I still have thirty-five minutes left.

I try to get up but he holds me down for a moment before he lets me go.

"Where are you going?" he asks.

"I just want to get out of this," I say, drawing my hands across the bodice of my dress, "so we can really relax. Can I put on some music?"

"If you want," he says. He seems peeved at my tactics, but resigned.

I find a jazz station on the radio and let my dress fall, stepping out of the heap when it ends up on the floor. My instinct is to run into the bathroom but I close my eyes and imagine myself a mysterious burlesque performer. I start dancing, run my hands over my bra, my stomach, my hips, and shake my hair across my back.

"Why don't you help me get out of this stuff," Scott says.

I had forgotten that his getting naked was part of the bargain. I'm glad for the time it takes to undo the buttons on his shirt; his breath on my chest is impatient. His nose hairs need clipping and there is a fleck of something stuck in his bottom teeth, which are now at eye level. I tell myself that he is just a person, flawed and needy, good and bad, deserving of compassion and affection. And that he picked me, out of all the others in the world.

He smells like musky cologne and he gives off heat, his skin only inches from mine. I touch his chest lightly with both my hands, as if there were the chance of an electric shock. It's like petting an unfamiliar animal; alive, pulsing, foreign. I'm glad he's not too hairy and maintains the nicely shaped body of a once-physical man. This is not so bad at all. This could be a drunken blind date that is going too far. If only I were drunk. When I kneel next to him, Scott slides down toward horizontal and closes his hands around my wrists, pressing my hands firmly against him. He has working hands, rough and blunt, veined and strong, and I feel a flicker, not of attraction but of nerves. I am now the animal—small, timid, and rabbitlike vulnerable.

"You feel great," I say. "So strong."

My tone is wooden but he hears what he wants to hear. I move my hands in languid circles and he eases his grip. I wish he would close his eyes—it would make it easier for me to perform—but he keeps them riveted on me.

"Hi, beautiful," he says softly as he puts his hand on the side of my face, and vicelike, moves it until it cradles my skull, and pulls my resistant head to his, his open mouth waiting. The kiss feels flat and uncharged, his lips chapped from dry Utah air and his tongue feral as he licks my lips and gropes into my mouth. This is an experiment, I try to convince myself, and it's really no worse than kissing Rob Thurman in the ninth grade with his spit-filled mouth acrid from dip. At least Scott tastes like toothpaste. At least he is not trying to get halfway down my throat.

But as soon as the thought passes, his oral assault becomes more frenzied and his tongue jabs straight back as far as it can into my mouth. I try to hide a reflexive gag that makes my eyes water. I pull away to regain some bearings.

"Hey, slow down there," I say. "Let me change positions so I'm not all twisted around."

"Yeah. Okay, yeah. You're right." Scott's eyes are heavy-lidded as he undoes his belt. "Take off my pants. I want to feel you."

This is entirely voluntary, I think, and I am choosing to take off a stranger's pants even though I don't want them to be off. I unbutton and unzip his chinos, my hand alarmingly grazing his erection under his blue plaid boxers. He lifts up so I can pull his pants off.

I don't have a lot of options left. I straddle him and his mouth and hands are everywhere. It's almost acrobatic trying to monitor what's going where. I wish the lights were off but that might make it easier for him to transgress. He's about to unhook my bra, his breathing hard and determined, but I grab his hands.

"No, baby. You know the rules."

Without comment he drops the task and begins to massage my buttocks with vigorous kneading. I gyrate on his lap like I have seen the strippers do, simulating sex, simulating everything. It's a curious thing to be acting out these steps without any sparks urging me forward. It doesn't feel bad exactly, but it feels impartial and distant. I suck on his neck, wanting to give him a hickey as a memento. He rubs my breasts through my bra as I roll around on top of him.

"I want to see you touch yourself," I say. "I want to watch you."

This is not legal for me to say, but I want to do this for Scott because he's my first and I know he's not a cop. He reaches inside his underwear, and as he watches me writhe around the bed through half-closed eyes, he gulps and moans. I smile and move faster.

*

The only time I have ever slept with someone I didn't really know was the first night I met McCallister. We had been set up by a friend of mine from work, and all I knew of him was that he was tall, neurotic, strawberry blond, and funny. We met at a dark and uncrowded little nook of a bar with overstuffed booths that enveloped us in instant intimacy. We discussed the merits of different breakfast cereals, whether *Hud* was cooler than *The Hustler*, the hotness quotient of various pop-star vixens. We drank, we smoked, we laughed. It was easy and I liked him straight away—his squint, his square-tipped fingers, his incessant self-deprecation, his charming laugh. He had a sureness in the way he asked me questions, held his beer, chatted with the bartender, put his hand briefly on my back on the way out the door, but he also had a childlike need for affirmation on things as small as the way he parted his hair. The combination got me.

We walked the fifteen blocks to his apartment on the pretense of watching a movie. I felt young and drunk and sanguine. It was early June, before the unbearable, heavy heat of the city in summer, and McCallister took my hand with instinctive ease, as if we'd been dating for years. He stopped for beer and cigarettes and M&Ms at the corner store. We started to make out as soon as the elevator doors closed.

It wasn't that I was overwhelmingly attracted to McCallister. It's more that there wasn't anything wrong with him— no embarrassing political remarks, no troubling tics, no evidence of trying too hard, no warning signals for possible land mines. He wasn't cheap, belligerent, effeminate, overly earnest, loud, conservative, strident, cynical, arrogant, or recently dumped. There were no cringe moments. He made me laugh. He thought I was smart. I liked his smell. He was a great kisser. One night with McCallister, and I exhaled and settled in.

*

When Scott is finished, I reach over him and click off the radio. An intensified silence follows and I'm aware of the creak of the mattress, the sound of my breathing, the drip in the shower, a police siren. The room has surrendered itself to calm. I help Scott wipe off his stomach with a wet washcloth; I feel like I'm playing nurse, generously administering to a patient. However false the moment is, I feel a closeness, even though the moment is more foreign than any before it. I slide under the covers and Scott rubs my arm, back and forth with soft strokes as I lie on his chest. He tells me about the first time he went deer hunting with his dad and how connected he felt to everything. He says that he is almost embarrassed sometimes about how much he likes his job, being in charge and building things. He wonders how he came to be a man of thirty-seven when he still feels the same as he did in high school. I am paid to be the listener and the giver, to have no needs of my own.

The ring of the phone is jarring intruder. I rise from the bed to answer it, grabbing my dress from the floor along the way.

And now there is no pretext of half-truth or excuse, no quiet resentment, no need to pretend it was something it wasn't. Scott tips me $50 on top of the $120. I wonder whether he will want to see me another time or if in our pseudo-consummation he discovered everything he wanted to know. I have a feeling he will never call again.

"That was fun," he says. "You can stay and hang out if you want. I mean, I don't know. Get some food. Watch a movie. I have this place for the night. Just casual, you know?"

"I have to get going," I say. "But thanks. It was nice to meet you. Maybe I'll see you again sometime."

I pull my coat over my unzipped dress, and all at once can't get my shoes on fast enough.

"Roxanne?"

"Yeah?" I ask, barely disguising my haste.

"I know this was work and everything. But if you ever want to play some golf, grab a drink or something." He knows the answer even while he asks. I admire his optimism. He looks away and searches for the remote control.

"Oh, um. Scott. Thanks. But…"

"No, totally. Just wanted to, you know, put it out there."

He clicks on the TV and stares at the History Channel, appearing to be captivated by Winston Churchill.

"Okay, then. Bye. I'll see you," I say, "around."

I head for the door in a trot.

A man in a gray cashmere sweater holds the elevator door for me when he sees me coming.

"Thanks," I say, attempting to straighten my undone dress and get oxygen to my brain.

"You're welcome," he says, with the slightest of smiles.

We watch the lights of descending floors. I sniffle but I don't care enough to scrounge for a tissue in my purse. I'm afraid to think about anything, in case this man can sense the nature of my thoughts. I concentrate on my fingernails and clench the inside of my cheek with my teeth.

"On your way out?" he asks, as we stop on the fifth floor. No one gets on.

"Not exactly," I say.

From the side of his face I'd guess he was forty. He's well-groomed with a fading tan.

"I'm in from San Diego," he says. "For work. Do you know where I might go for a drink around here?"

Because he only glances at me when he asks this, and because he doesn't have a coat with him as if he had planned on going out, and because of something about the way he clamps his lips together as if to cover a sure-of-himself grin, it crosses my mind that he thinks I am a prostitute. And for this I want to ask him what he's really asking, to humiliate him, to make him feel small.

"I don't know," I say instead. "I'm afraid you're on your own."

When the doors open to the lobby, I step out in front of him without looking back. I just need to make it to the car, count the steps, breathe deeply, focus on the pattern of the marble floor, but as soon as the cold air hits my face, a tear escapes in a loose, warm rivulet down my cheek.

"Watch that sidewalk there, ma'am," the doorman says. "Someone fell already. The ice is invisible."

I wonder if he knows.

"Thanks," I say. "Good night."

"Good night, dear," he says.

It occurs to me that I might see this man again and again, different nights, different dresses. He will watch me get older. Fantasize about me. Pity me.

But by the time I make it to the car, I have conquered the need to cry. I did it. The heater blows hard and dry, and I realize I'm starving. I drive to 700 South and the fast-food strip, pull into the drive-through at Dunkin' Donuts and order a half dozen assorted. I drive east up the hill toward the university, turning at random on quiet streets until most of the donuts are gone, and then I wend my way back to the Avenues and my apartment.

Through the window I can see Ember curled up on Ford's lap in the dancing blue light of the TV, and Ralf asleep near their feet.

chapter 10

I awake at dawn to find Ralf asleep on my bedroom floor using my bathrobe as a blanket and a towel as a pillow, his hands tucked under his chin. He must have slipped in during the night.

"Ralf," I whisper. "Ralf."

"Oh, hi. Sorry," he says, rubbing his eyes. "I know I should have asked if I could sleep in here but I didn't want to wake you to see if it was okay. I didn't want to be a third wheel out there."

"It's okay," I say. "Why don't you move up here?"

I know that he is too shy to ever make any kind of move, and I really want the company.

"No, no. I'm fine. I have to get up soon anyway."

"Ralf, it's not even six. And it's Saturday. Come on."

He yawns, then scrambles up onto the bed in his jeans and T-shirt, curls away from me on the far edge, and pulls up the covers. I scoot over and hug his body into mine to glean his warmth, to feel his realness, his familiar and gentle presence. The smell of smoke and winter lingers in his hair.

"I was having this dream where you guys were all trying to stuff things in my suitcase when I wasn't looking," he says.

"That's pretty funny," I say.

"It was more them than you. I didn't mind it really. We were getting ready for an earthquake or something."

Ralf extricates himself from me and the blankets and raises himself up onto his elbows.

"Did you know that the church is so primed for Armageddon that they've been stockpiling dried grain under the city for thirty years?" he asks.

"Grain can last that long?"

"I don't know. Maybe they have special airtight silos. I wouldn't doubt it if there is a whole parallel city down there. It's pretty awesome that they're so prepared."

"What did you do last night?" I ask.

I venture my hand to his chest but he ignores it and falls back into the pillow. I decide to leave him alone and inch away toward my side of the bed.

"Played rummy with my uncle," he says. "And watched a *Hogan's Heroes* marathon."

I admire Ralf for his truthfulness. He never tries to play it cool.

"Ember and Ford swung by and picked me up on the way back from gambling. You sneaked in pretty quietly last night."

"Yeah," I say.

"Long night at the office?"

"Something like that," I say.

The early sun starts to make itself known through the blinds, filling the room with diffuse, gray light. But it's still too much too soon and I hook my arm across my eyes.

"Do you think Ember's going to go with him?" I ask. "With Ford?"

"I don't know. He keeps asking her, you know. He must have asked her ten times last night. She says no sometimes and yes sometimes but never with much conviction either way. It's a weird game they play."

"I've gotten used to having them around," I say.

"Man. It's sure going to suck when Ford goes," he says.

"Yeah," I say. "You could probably go down to Moab with him if you wanted."

"I've thought about it. But what would I do there? I don't know so much about the river. Besides, there's this construction job starting in a couple weeks in West Valley City. It'll be me and a bunch of Tongans."

I roll over to face him; his profile comes into relief with the light. I want him to move toward me and take over the moment.

"Ralf?"

"Yeah?"

"I'm not tired."

"Me neither," he says.

"So what should we do about it?"

"How about breakfast?" he says. "I'm starving."

We drive out east into the mouth of Emigration Canyon, and although there is considerable snow covering the benches of the valley, the roads are clear. The morning cold dissipates as Ralf plays the Waylon Jennings tape he took from Ford's truck. It's a sharply lit morning, the sun gaining momentum as it rises, and blinding glints reflect off the icy top layer of snow. Last night at the hotel has the hazy edges of a daydream. I can barely conjure Scott's face. Ralf watches out his window, tapping his fingers on his knees.

"Is it lonely living out there in Tooele?" I ask.

"Probably no more so than anywhere else. My cousin's basement can be cold and depressing sometimes but that's why I come hang out with you guys."

"Do you think you'll ever leave here?" I ask.

"Utah? No way. It's home. I belong to it. It may seem like everyone is conforming here but conformity is no way the same thing as being normal. This is probably one of the most unnormal places there is. And that's good. Don't you think?"

We slowly gain altitude as we snake farther into the winding canyon, around the jagged rock faces, the horse camp, the random houses set deep within the trees. The aspens are bare but the pines are a rich blue-green in the frosty mist the sun hasn't yet been able to reach.

"This is what I love about Salt Lake," I say. "Within minutes we're here." I point my hand in an arc across the windshield to span the rugged beauty on all sides.

Ralf smiles and nods.

"When I was a kid, I used to feel sorry for the kids on TV who lived in big cities," he says. "I thought anyone who lived there was poor and that's why they couldn't leave. All that cement and chain-link fences. All those locks on the doors. Graffiti. Not that I think that now. I mean, I know that people like it there, that there's cool stuff and all. I guess."

"It has its charms," I say.

"Like that McDonald guy?"

"McCallister."

"Right, McCallister. But with or without good old McCallister, bet you can't see an eagle in the Big Apple," he says, stabbing the air with his finger.

"You got me there," I say.

Ruth's neon sign comes into view as we round the curve of a protruding canyon wall. The old diner is parked in the middle of the trees and granite, as if it just got tired en route, stopped to rest and never left. For sixty years Ruth herself cooked up breakfast for the hunters, the travelers, the fringe, the outsiders. Although most people who come here actually drive out from Salt Lake City, Ruth's is decidedly un-Mormon in its feel. There's no blond, apple-cheeked waitstaff or automatic cheer. There is a sense that people take a respite from their lives here, that they use time at Ruth's to regroup. We park next to a pickup laden with rifles and hunting gear, emblazoned with mud-and-salt-caked bumper stickers. The single legible one reads, "I love animals. They are delicious."

We're ahead of the morning rush. The only customers are a group of camouflaged hunters hunched over their coffee at a table in the far corner, shoveling eggs into their mouths between periodic comments. As soon as we sit, the waiter, a scruffy guy Ford has pointed out as an off-season river guide, appears with coffee and I give myself over to the promising smells of bacon and biscuits. Prickly warmth darts around my body, and then it settles like a blanket around my shoulders. Feeling soothed and languorous, I almost tell Ralf what I was really doing last night. In this light it seems merely exotic. But a quick look at his childlike bed-head and his wrinkled flannel shirt and I decide against it. I know he would be disappointed to the core.

"Did you know that the church keeps track of inactive members?" he asks.

I welcome the resumption of our Mormon dialogue, as if we'd been talking about it all along.

"'Inactive' meaning 'not Mormon anymore'?"

"Mormon but not churchgoing. Jack Mormon. Like me. No matter where I happen to be living, even the time I went to live in the Ozarks, every few months I'll answer the phone and some smiley guy will say, 'Brother Lundgren?' It's really quite amazing. The FBI should get in on that action."

"I wouldn't like that at all. I like the idea of being

where no one can find me. That it's possible to slip away if I wanted to, without explanation, to do things no one knows about but me."

"Really? I think it's reassuring to know someone always knows were I am. It gives me credibility or something. It means I exist in a larger context. Anyway, it's not like you can get rid of them just because they don't know where you are. And it's not like McCallister doesn't keep tabs on you anyway."

The river guide returns and we order enough pancakes and bacon and hash browns for four, and then Ralf enacts the Mormon sales pitch he used while on his mission in Amsterdam. I take in every word, watch the expressions on his face, encourage him to talk and talk. The longer I keep it going, the more time I have in this fragile, contented haze. He tells me about the still, small voice of the Lord as revealed to Joseph Smith, and how Mormons are taught to listen for it, to develop their own relationship with God. When the food arrives, I take small bites and chew slowly, trying to keep the regret about last night from taking hold, shoving those thoughts to the periphery. Plied with coffee, Ralf goes and goes. I missed the segue but he is now talking about the church's recent anti-sin campaigns.

"Last year they proposed a bill in the state legislature that would have outlawed public ashtrays," Ralf says, "so kids couldn't scrounge for butts. And up in Bountiful? All the magazines, even, like, the women's fashion ones, are covered up except for the titles. As if just the sight of a beautiful woman will incite impure thoughts. Which I suppose may be the case but you can't regulate thoughts and behavior in that way. That's where church leaders go wrong. Moral micromanagement turns people off."

The hunters pass behind me, their boots squeaking on the linoleum floor.

"That's just beautiful," I hear one of them say in an all-too-familiar voice.

I turn as they leave, just in time to see longish ash-blond hair escaping from underneath a baseball cap. Scott slaps one of the guys on the back and laughs as they push through the front door and disappear into the morning glare. He didn't see me. The feeling of getting away with it bubbles up in me and transforms into a heady giddiness.

But then the door opens and Scott ducks back in. I quickly look down but it doesn't matter because he looks past me. I don't register. A ponytail and a different context is all the disguise I need. He grabs his vest off the back of the chair and exits once again.

My heart slows to normal. I made Scott happy and then I disappeared.

"Are you going to eat that piece of bacon?" Ralf asks.

"It's all yours," I say.

I slather raspberry jam onto a biscuit. I feel powerful with expanded possibilities.

*

McCallister calls as I am draped across Ember on the couch, my feet in her lap. It was daytime when we arranged ourselves; no one bothered to turn on the lights as it sank into dusk.

"So how was it?" McCallister asks.

"How was what?" I ask, my pulse quickening.

"Your date."

"Oh. Fine. It was okay."

"Are you going to see this mystery guy again?"

"Probably not," I say.

McCallister lets my evasiveness go without comment. A salt truck rumbles outside and swallows his words.

"What?" I ask.

"Maria has decided to paint the apartment in varying shades of red. What do you think about that?" he asks. "Do you think it's some kind of statement?"

"We won't be able to hang out like this if I go to Moab," Ember says.

"What?" McCallister asks.

"That's Ember," I say.

"You haven't answered my question," he says.

"Here's a question," I say. "How come you call me so much when another woman is painting your walls?"

"Go Jane," Ember says, squeezing my foot.

"Because we're friends," McCallister says, his voice wounded and whiny at the same time. "Friends talk, they ask advice, they laugh together. Are you saying we're not friends?"

I don't say anything.

"I don't like talking to you when other people are around," he says.

My toughness recedes. The thought of his calling my bluff, withdrawing from me, leaves me feeling frightened and ill-equipped.

"I think red might look all right," I say, backing down. "I don't think it has to mean you're losing your identity or anything."

"But it might make me look sallow," he says.

"What's he saying?" Ember asks.

"Something about his complexion," I say.

"He's such a girl," she says.

"What?" McCallister asks.

"Nothing," I say.

"Okay. I guess red it is. Might spice it up a bit in here. I'll call you later, Jane. I like it better when I get you all to myself," he says.

"Don't pout," I say. I hang up and let the phone fall to the carpet.

It's all the way dark. I sit up next to Ember.

"I have something to tell you," I say.

Ember's eyes glow in the streetlight shining through the window.

"Meet the newest Utah escort."

"Jane!" she says, grasping my hands between hers. "We're so the same."

When I look up, it takes me a moment to notice Ford

leaning in the doorway in the dark. I don't know how long he's been there but by his crossed arms and the slight shaking of his head, I know he has heard enough.

chapter 11

Nikyla, sitting on the arm of one of the office love seats, has the bulb of a lamp aimed at Diamond's face and is plucking her eyebrows for her.

"I feel like shit. I hate going out when I have my period," Diamond says.

"Stop moving. It's hard to get these tiny ones," Nikyla says, stretching the arch of Diamond's brow taut.

"Hi, girls," I say.

"Well, well, well," Nikyla says. "Is it true?"

I laugh.

"I think I hear hell freezing over," Diamond says.

Nikyla stands and holds her arms open and wraps me up in a hug.

"I came to check the schedule. Do my write-up," I say.

"Welcome to the jungle," Diamond says. "Hey, help me work on these," she says to Nikyla, her hands on her enhanced breasts as if they were not attached to her body. "They're getting all hard and shit."

Nikyla takes one of Diamond's breasts between her hands.

"Okay. How about this," Nikyla says, "Roxanne. Age twenty-six, slender, long dark hair, brown eyes. 35-24-33, smart, sensual, a great listener. A real beauty."

"In my wildest fantasies," I say.

"Oh please. Like it matters. It's perfect. You'll attract the ones who are looking for love." Nikyla takes Diamond's other breast in her hands and rolls it with her palms.

"Great," I say. "Just what I need."

"Hey, Rox, I can't find Jezebel. She's flaking again," Kendra says from the office between mouthfuls of Pringles. "Want to be on?"

"Uh, okay," I say. "Sure. I better go home and shower. Get gussied up."

"Cinderella off to the ball," Diamond says.

Nikyla smiles at me, mouths "good luck," and blows me a kiss.

I like how escorting blots out reality, one hour at a time, and I'm secretly excited to get back out there.

*

Ember's car won't start, so on the way to my date I drive her down to Holladay to the house of this guy she's already seen three times in two weeks. She just says he's kind of in love with her and tips big, but my guess is that he's her cocaine connection. She seems to have an endless supply these days. I find white powder on every smooth surface of the house.

"So what's the deal with art school?" I ask. "Are you going to start in the spring?"

I want her to have a concrete reason to stay in Salt Lake with me. Something to ground her here. Her wildness scares me even as I crave its glow, its intensity.

"I don't know. Yeah, I guess," she says. "It depends, you know?"

Ember lights another cigarette with the butt of the one she's still smoking.

"You could probably take extension classes at the U in the meantime if you wanted, like drawing or painting. I was thinking about taking some kind of class. Want to go up there tomorrow with me and check it out?"

"I don't think I can handle classes right now," Ember says, blowing out smoke and rubbing her nose with rabid persistence. "But you should, Janie. You're smart. I think that would be great for you. Turn left at the light."

I park in front of a sagging, putty-colored ranch house with a corrugated metal fence and an old washing machine poking up through the snow on the lawn.

"Are you sure he's home? There aren't any lights on," I say.

"It trips him out to have on a lot of lights. He's probably in the basement. Don't worry. He's a pussycat. I'll cab home."

Mohammed would be furious to see that she's going

out in jeans and an old "Wisconsin" sweatshirt under her ski jacket.

"Okay," I say. "Be careful."

"Hey, good luck tonight," she says.

"Thanks," I say.

"Remember, they're all just men," she says. "Just act like you really like him. He'll sense it and reward you for it. And however it goes, know that the guy's lucky to get you."

She gives me a kiss, her breath a mix of cherry cough drops and smoke, and opens the door. Before shutting it, she leans back in.

"I'm not going to go," she says. Her eyes simmer.

"You're not?"

"I mean with Ford. I'm not going to Moab," she says.

"Oh, I'm so glad," I say. I'm flooded with selfish relief and thrill. I won't be the one left behind.

"Yeah, it's going to be great," she says.

"Does Ford know?"

"Sort of," she says and slams the door.

Ember steps back, raises her arms out wide and looks at the sky as if to say "This kingdom is ours!" She giggles and drops her arms as she walks up to the dilapidated house. She goes in without knocking.

I'm on my way to see someone named Harold in South Sandy. Kendra said he sounded normal enough, if a tad nervous, and although we don't normally meet new clients at their houses, he pressed for an exception and it was the only way she could close the date.

Sandy is a flat, sprawling, middle-class suburb with young trees and one-story houses and a lot of big-portion chain restaurants. Harold's tidy brick house is at the end of the street, on a cul de sac, and it's easy to spot because it's the only one not strewn with Christmas lights. I wear a conservative outfit at his request, a tailored shirt and pinstriped pants with my hair pulled back. Because I heard he is skittish and his name is Harold, tonight I'm feeling emboldened. The short cement walkway from the driveway to the door has been shoveled clear with perfect precision. Shades are drawn over every window. The door knocker is the sharp-angled head of a watchful wolf. It's heavy and cold in my hand as I strike the brass plate on the door.

There are the muffled steps of stocking feet, a pause as he examines me through the peephole—I smile—and then the clicks of locks and chains being undone. The pale face that appears in the door is strikingly rectangular, accentuated by a boxy hairline and a deep side part.

"Yes?" he asks.

I can't tell if his slight accent is really British or some affectation.

"I'm Roxanne," I say, irritated that he hasn't immediately let me in from the winter night. The frosty wind nips my ankles.

"Oh," he says. "Yes." The door is still only open a foot or so. "I see. You'll have to take off your shoes out there, I'm afraid."

"Okay," I say. The cement landing sends deadening cold into my feet, and I stand like a flamingo trying to keep one of them warm. "Uh, may I come in?"

"Yes, of course," Harold says. He pauses before opening the door to allow my passage. "Let me take your coat."

The house has a worn sterility to it: no books, no magazines, no photographs, no tchotchkes. Nothing on the surfaces, and nothing out of place. There is a shabby institutional couch, its pillows perfectly aligned, an old Zenith television, dust-free and reflecting the room like a fishbowl, and a small black acrylic coffee table. The drab loden-colored carpet is flat, as if it had been recently shorn.

"Can I offer you some water?" he asks.

Harold stands with his hands on his thighs, leaning forward like a butler ready to serve. The fleshy lobes of his big ears, his ample nose, and his large, unruly hands seem incongruous in the sparse room, and Harold himself appears uncomfortable in his body.

"Yes, please," I say. "If it's no trouble."

I would guess from the lines on his face he is in his mid-fifties, though his old cardigan, trousers, and slippers give him a more elderly air.

As he shuffles off to the kitchen, I sit on the middle cushion of the couch—my self-assuredness receding—cross my legs, then uncross them, put my hands in my lap, then lace my fingers, without the slightest idea of how to act for this man.

"Your name again, miss?" he asks when he returns, handing me a glass.

"Roxanne."

"Well, Roxanne. I guess I'm supposed to pay you now, is that it?"

I smile and look down at my lap. From an old billfold, Harold pulls a stack of twenty-dollar bills; all facing the same way, all seemingly ironed, and hands them to me one at a time.

"You know I've never done this before," he says.

"Well then, Harold. I'm the lucky one," I say, trying hard to sound genuine. "I get to take you on your maiden voyage."

After I call in, we sit side by side on the couch without touching while I ask him questions about his job (book-keeper for an accountant), if he's married (no), if he has kids (no), where he's from (Pocatello, Idaho), about his hobbies (jigsaw puzzles, crossword puzzles, bird-watching). I look for clues in his demeanor about what to do next but he gives no hints, not even a raised eyebrow or a suggestive narrowing of his eyes.

"So, Harold," I say after fifteen minutes of polite chat-ting. I should just let the clock tick down but I feel like he's paying me to take the lead. "What would you like for me to do for you this evening?"

He squints and frowns, the parenthetical lines around his mouth slacken, but then he turns to me with a naughty grin.

"I've been so bad," he says. "And I think it is now time for my punishment."

He must have been too timid to reveal this predilection on the phone or else Kendra would have sent him S&M Samantha. Doing everything in my power to stifle a smile that threatens to spring up, I stand with my hands on my hips and act like I know exactly what I'm doing.

"Is it? Is it time?" he asks.

"Harold. Go to your room. Now." I point out of the living room. "I'll be back to deal with you in a minute."

"Should I crawl?" he asks, looking up at me with a demure downward tilt of his head.

"Yes," I say. "Of course you should."

In the kitchen I look for any nonlethal implements that might be put to use—a wooden spoon, a meat tenderizer, a tray of ice cubes, a rolling pin, a ball of string. I start laughing at my collection, and have to clear my throat with vigor to stop before I reach the bedroom.

Harold has stripped to his boxers, undershirt, and black socks, and he is on all fours on the floor at the foot of the bed. My first reaction is not that he looks ridiculous—he does—but that he is a sad man. I unload the kitchen utensils onto the bed; its threadbare quilt pulled taut with angular, military-style corners. I opt for the spoon, slapping it against my palm.

"Good boy, for doing as you were told. But that doesn't mean you're off the hook," I say.

I nudge down one side of his underwear, exposing the almost translucent flesh of his left buttock cheek. I graze the skin with my fingers before landing a light smack with the wooden spoon. And again, harder, turning his pale skin pink. Another crack of the spoon and a low, animal-like moan escapes from him. The meat tenderizer proves trickier, as it bounces off his butt. I order his shirt off and drag the jagged head of the mallet against his back.

Harold says, "Oh, oh, oh," with the slow rhythm of a mantra, so I gather I'm doing what he wants. He doesn't open his eyes or move away.

Before the ice melts on the bed, I take the tray and hold it to the soles of his feet, for lack of any better idea, and he starts and whimpers but I hold the ice steady, amazed that he is paying me for this.

"I know I deserve it," he says. "Make me pay. Make me suffer."

I pull his boxers down to his knees and slap him as hard as I can muster, leaving my palm stinging. I slap him again and again. His skin quivers with the blows. With each hit I feel more in control and invigorated. Adrenaline surges through my veins. It is as if a part of me has come out of hibernation, and I welcome it.

"I want to see you crawl, Harold. Like the big baby you are," I say. "Crawl!"

He obeys, crawling on his hands and knees in a circle, looking over his shoulder at me with that big, square face of his, with the fear and bafflement of a toddler, and I wonder if I'm damaging this man forever. He scoots around the perimeter of the room and I use the spoon like a riding crop each time he passes by. His knees are rug-burned. His forehead is damp.

"Stop," I shout. "Now go to the corner and don't move until I say so.

Harold wedges himself against the corner walls, his boxers tangled up around his knees. Red striations run down the length of his back. I kneel behind him and rake my fingernails across his shoulders.

"Don't you dare turn around," I whisper. "I mean it."

"I promise," he says. His breathing is quick and rasping.

Just as I claw my nails into his skin, Harold ejaculates onto the wall. And then I'm startled by the sight of tiny droplets of blood beading up within the finger-wide scratches on his back.

"Oh my god. I'm so sorry," I say. "I didn't mean to hurt you. Let me get something to clean you off."

"It's okay," Harold says. "Really."

When the phone rings, I answer it.

"You have five minutes," Kendra says.

By the time I hang up, Harold is zipping up his pants and his countenance has regained its former imperviousness.

"Thank you," he says, and extends his hand for me to shake it.

"You're welcome," I say, no longer in command, "I'm sorry about…I hope it was enjoyable for you."

"Yes," he says, "quite."

He pulls open his wallet and hands me a smooth twenty. I feel bad taking more of his money but I know he would feel worse if I tried to give it back. I want to ask him what exactly he is paying me for, if it's the only way he can find solace, if he's always been alone, where he finds joy, if he feels worse now that it's over, if he thinks I pity him or if he cares.

I want to give Harold a hug, but that's not an option. He helps me put on my coat, then swiftly leads the way down the hall to the door.

"Good night," I say. "Thank you."

He looks past me at the brightly lit houses of his neighbors.

"I like your door knocker," I say.

The side of his mouth curls in the tiniest upturn.

I slip into my cold shoes on the landing. As I step down onto the little path, I hear the multitude of locks clack with a satisfying finality behind me.

For so long I have felt a constricting mantle of fear and limitation. But now I sense it ease. I feel like a ball of rubber bands, and that one more has just been peeled away.

chapter 12

When I get up the next morning, I find Ford swaddled in a Mexican serape on the floor leaning against the couch. He gives me a straight-lipped attempt at a smile and I feel distanced from him in a way that I've never felt before. Despite my justifications, I can't shake the sense of having betrayed him. We haven't even discussed the escorting—that being my thing with Ember. I fill the coffee pot with water.

"Hey, Jane?"

"Yeah?" My breath quickens at the threat of a confrontation I'm not ready for.

"You know you really should think about giving up coffee," he says. "It's bad for you."

This from a guy whose girlfriend has a serious cocaine habit.

"Uh huh," I say, avoiding his veiled instigation.

"It's not like we're eighteen anymore."

"Where's the missus?" I ask.

"We got in a fight this morning. I suppose she told

you she's not going with me."

"She mentioned it last night."

"She's all yours now," he says. His eyes shine in the reflection of the window.

I'm both excited and contrite about this prospect. I pour a cup of coffee mid-brew and the machine drips and spatters until I return the pot. I sit next to Ford and cover my legs with the ratty blanket.

"Maybe it's the best thing for now," I say.

He gives a skeptic snort.

"Where'd she go anyway?" I ask.

He shrugs. His eyes, which have always looked impossibly young, are red-rimmed and have gray-blue circles beneath them.

"I guess it's not so easy having a crazy girlfriend," I say.

A huge icicle hangs precariously from the rain gutter and drips a determined stream against the side of the window.

"We don't talk anymore," he says, "I mean, you and me."

"I've been busy," I say.

"So you have."

I sip my coffee. It's watery and too hot.

"I'm sorry," I say.

"Are you?" he asks.

I look down into my mug and feel the steam on my face.

He breathes out through puffed cheeks.

"I have an idea. Let's take a walk," he says.

It's another bright day infused with a false sense of impending spring. We walk down to First South and turn west toward downtown, dodging falling chunks of snow from the canopy of oak tree branches above the sidewalk. I hold Ford's hand, cracked and rough from working on the house in the cold. I wait for him to talk.

"I'm tired out, Jane," he says at last. "I'm tired of us. You. Me. Ember. Ralf."

"Even Ralf?"

"He's part of the mess."

"What do you mean?"

"Oh come on. He's so clearly in love with you," Ford says, dropping my hand. "He speaks of you with this reverent praise. But I wouldn't want to be the one to tell him about your change of career."

My face is hot. I feel the weight of my body drain into my feet.

"I knew he had a crush," I say meekly. "But what was I supposed to do, not be his friend?"

"You could start by not cultivating his adoration. I'm sure it feels nice to be the object of it, but have some mercy. It's not like you don't have McCallister to fawn over you."

I am stung by his hostility.

"Huh," I say, trying not to cry. "That means a lot coming from someone as evolved as you."

Ford steps off the sidewalk into the snow to let a couple with a double stroller pass. I keep walking. And then walk faster, wanting to leave him behind.

"Jane," he says. "What are you doing?"

I don't answer.

"Wait," he says, jogging to catch up with me.

I turn away and dab at my eyes. I'm angry but something in Ford's biting encapsulation resonates and fills me with shame.

"Hey. I'm sorry," he says. "Stop for a second, will you?"

"Since when did you become so judgmental?" I ask, crossing my arms across my chest.

"I take it back," he says. "Okay?"

I sniffle and rummage for a tissue in my pockets. Ford hands me a bandanna.

"Thanks," I say blowing my nose.

"I'm just upset," he says. "Everyone else's problems seem so much easier to solve than my own."

I offer him back his handkerchief and we laugh and I put in my pocket.

He takes my hand. I let him. We resume walking together toward the granite spires in a tenuous truce.

"I'll tell Ralf about the escorting," I say.

"Maybe you should," he says. "Or maybe you shouldn't. I don't know."

We cross over to the sunny side of the street and walk past the tuxedo rental store and the violin-making workshop.

"More violins are produced here than in any other

city outside of Vienna," I say.

"I'm leaving the day after tomorrow," Ford says.

This is not a surprise but it brings with it a sudden realization that Ford may be my last link to rationality, that his presence has the power to make everything normal again.

"Maybe you should stay," I say too softly, unable to commit to being reeled into safety.

"I have to make sure the trailer hasn't been carried off by a pack of wild coyotes," he says.

The promise of the post-Ford unknown with Ember is both scary and seductive. I fear what I crave.

"You should take Ralf with you down to Moab," I say.

"You wish," Ford says, putting his arm around my shoulders,

We walk through the immense iron gates of Temple Square into the well-manicured grounds. Camera-toting Mormon tourists snap away at the tabernacle, the temple, the ecclesiastical murals in the visitors' center. Young tour guides in shin-length skirts and long coats crisscross the square with their smiling groups in tow.

"I know she has a problem," Ford says. "But I don't think there's anything I can do about it. She's impossible to get to. I think I've gotten in and then all of a sudden, she slips away again."

"Yeah, but that's also what you love about her," I say.

Invisible speakers around the square broadcast Mormon hymns at near-subliminal levels, noticeable only when the wind stops. The accompaniment makes the square feel like a religious shopping mall.

"So why are you doing the escorting thing anyway?" he asks. "What's that about?"

"You're the one who suggested it to me in the first place, remember?"

"I was just showing off. Trying to provoke you," he says. "I didn't really think you'd do it."

The block of Main Street the church purchased from the city is as neat and contained as a Parisian park. We stop at a bench and Ford lights us each a cigarette, smoking being a habit he has adopted since arriving in Salt Lake.

"You shouldn't worry about my moral compass," I say.

He shrugs. "That doesn't answer my question."

"Have you ever felt like who you are isn't really who you are?"

"Huh?"

"I mean that the you that goes about your day is incongruous with the real idea of you that you've lost track of?"

I'm interrupted by a freckle-faced teenager with a skateboard under his arm who stands in front of us, the sun like a halo behind his head.

"Excuse me, folks," he says.

I make a visor with my hand to see him. "Yes?"

"No smoking here, I'm afraid," he says, pointing to a

small sign in a flowerpot a few feet away.

"We're outside," Ford says. "It's Main Street, for god's sake."

"Just the rules," the kid says. He stays until we have stubbed out the cigarettes, then picks up the butts from the ground and tosses them into the trash can.

"Have yourselves a pleasant day," he says. He drops his skateboard and rolls away.

"I have to get to work, anyway," I say.

Ford sighs. "Well, I guess I'll see you later."

*

After her latest disappearance, Jezebel has resurfaced and watches *Judge Judy* as Albee bites the ankles of her jeans and scampers after a tennis ball under the couch.

"Hey," I say, happy to see she's alive. "Where've you been?"

"Around," she says. "I heard the big news. You slut."

She takes the gooey ball from the puppy and throws it at me. I dodge it and laugh.

"Albee has gotten bigger, I think," I say.

"Do you want him? I can't deal anymore. Not that he isn't so cute." She grabs his muzzle and kisses him. "Cuter than the ass-face I had to see this morning."

"Watch your language," Mohammed says, the door slamming behind him. "This is a place of business."

The dog barks from under the couch.

"I will not tell you again," Mohammed says, pointing

at Jezebel. "Do not bring that animal here." He sneezes three times in a row. "I mean it. You are on the thin ice, young lady."

Mohammed touches my shoulder with his finger. "So being an escort is not such a horrible thing now?"

"It's okay," I say.

"Oh, you have a strip-o-gram tomorrow. In the police outfit."

Jezebel laughs but I am stupefied. Strip-o-grams are so rare I haven't even considered the possibility. The humiliation rises in my throat.

"Mohammed, please," I say with growing urgency. "You have to get someone else."

"Don't even look over here," Jezebel says.

"You will do it," he says to me. "And that is it." He erupts into another series of sneezes. "Take that dog away now!"

Jezebel gives him a mock salute, and when he turns, she rolls up her middle finger from her fist before she scoops up a squirming Albee and makes for the door.

The phone rings and Mohammed retreats into the back room.

"Good evening," I answer. "How may I help you?"

"I'll take double D, nice ass, redhead."

"McCallister. I can't talk now."

"Are you avoiding me?"

"What gave you that idea? Moving to Utah?"

"I mean it. When can we talk then?"

"Tomorrow I guess. Call me at home."

"Have you become some guy's ninth wife?"

"Not yet," I say.

"You're getting weirder, Jane. I'm worried."

Mohammed storms back in yelling in Arabic on his cell phone. He snaps the phone closed and puts his hands against the desk to steady himself, breathing noisily through his mouth.

"I think I am getting high blood pressure," he says. He places his hands on his chest like a grieving soprano, then leaves without another word.

chapter 13

I am sent on my first double with Jezebel to a new client, in for the night from San Francisco, at the Marriott across from the convention center. On the way to the hotel, Jezebel bounces around in the car like a giddy schoolgirl on the way to a dance. I feel like the chaperone. Albee yips in the backseat.

With his mustache and bushy mullet haircut, the guy doesn't look like he's from San Francisco. He's both lewd and jumpy, stammering as he says, "You girls'll have to fight over who gets me." Jezebel emits a truncated courtesy laugh, then turns to me and rolls her eyes. He undresses immediately and sits on the bed, his legs splayed, hair everywhere. Jezebel whoops and starts to dance. She takes my hand and spins in, kisses me on the neck, and spins out.

There is something off about this guy. He's shifty and forced in his interactions with us. His words don't match his face.

"Come on, you two, suck me," he says, looking at the

floor but holding his penis.

My disgust must register on my face because Jezebel swats my butt then grinds against me with her pelvis. I dance with uneasy halfheartedness as I take off my coat, then my sweater.

Jezebel is mesmerizing in her abandon. She's already down to her underwear—polka-dotted—and matching bra, making full use of the room space. One minute she's jumping on the bed and the next she's bending backward over him. I might as well not be in the room at all.

"Come on, Roxanne, join in," she says in a Betty Boop falsetto. She lifts my shirt over my head, then unzips my pants and peels them to the floor.

"Yeah, take it all off," he says, rubbing himself.

I catch him quickly glance at the window.

"Come on, little girl," he says to Jezebel. "Don't you want to feel it?"

"Oh, you're so big and hard," she says, reaching over to him on the bed.

"Jezebel," I say, but she is already moving her hand up and down his penis. I stand and watch, mute and ineffectual. One minute, then two. He looks at me when he ejaculates.

Before Jezebel has even wiped the semen off her hand, the man reaches for his pants, and something metallic catches the light.

"You're under arrest," he says.

*

Jezebel gets busted for indecent sexual contact. I follow the police car to the city jail, and three hours later, I hand over my credit card to pay her $500 fine.

"Hey," I say. She walks to me, her jacket pulled tightly across her chest.

"You can't tell on me, Rox. I'm already on Mohammed's shit list. I need this job," she says.

Her makeup is smeared beneath her eyes, making them look sunken. Her usually blown-straight blond bob is frizzed up like that of an unkempt doll. I take her arm as we go out into the night.

"I won't," I say. "Don't worry."

It's 1:30 a.m. and downtown is quiet except for the click of changing streetlights.

"I'll pay you back," Jezebel says. "I swear."

I know she won't but paying for her feels like I'm doing a good deed.

"What's the big deal anyway? What's the difference? The ending's the same; the guy gets off. It's a stupid law. So what if it's for money? So what if it makes me a prostitute? It's not hurting anyone."

Jezebel does what she's never done in front of me, she starts to cry, erupting in sniffly, hiccup-y tears she angrily tries to stop.

"He let me keep doing it. You saw him. That fuckhead. He took our money back."

"You should have asked him why his dick was so small, if it was some kind of birth defect," I say.

She giggles and wipes her eyes. I laugh too. I envy the way Jezebel's emotions are so close to the surface; they shift and bob from moment to moment like buoys on a choppy sea.

"I didn't have a clue he was a cop," she says.

We reach my car, where Albee has left drool and smudges all over the inside, and he's peed on the backseat.

"Sorry, Rox," Jezebel says. "Bad Albee. Bad dog."

His wagging tail thumps against the door as he licks her face. Jezebel turns on the radio to a pop station and mouths all the words to the song. She dances with the puppy's paws and joyously yells out the window at a group of young guys crossing the street toward Club DV8.

When I drop her at her car, Jezebel hops out like a sprite and waves back at me, and I wonder if it is just that simple for her to move on, not to dwell, examine, or dissect the meaning of her actions. I have a feeling she will fall asleep tonight as easily as any night. She dumps Albee into the Blazer—its left front bumper is still smashed—and she circles my car and peels out of the parking lot.

*

Just the thought of the polyester strip-o-gram outfit makes me recoil, though my protests don't carry much weight with Mohammed.

"The pants'll be too short. Complete floods," I say.

"No one will be looking at the pants," he says.

"It's a security guard's outfit, not a police uniform."

"Pfft," he says. "Oh, and I'll pay you after. It's a favor for this guy who bought two rugs. A bachelor party or some such thing for his friend."

"At three o'clock in the afternoon?"

"Does it matter?" he asks, raising his palms toward the ceiling.

Kendra snickers over at the desk, finishing off the last of her McRib.

"Don't worry, Rox," she says. "You'll actually *want* to take it off."

The pants are dark blue with flared cuffs that hover way above the tops of my black pumps, and they have a sharp perma-crease down the front. Their synthetic roughness makes my legs itch. They're so tight on top I have to lie flat on the floor to get the zipper up. The white polyester uniform shirt is big and wide with dirty cuffs I have to roll up, and a "security" patch on the sleeve in the shape of a shield. The hat looks like a Greek fisherman's hat, and all in all, I look like an asshole. I feel sick.

Kendra coughs on the powdered sugar of her mini donuts when I appear from the back and I snatch the Polaroid camera before her white-covered fingers can get it. She attempts to repress her smile, but I break first into teary laughter. I'm already distraught imagining the glare of daylight and the public ogling, without even a hotel room door against the outside world.

The building is in one of those flat, treeless business parks with one tinted-windowed cluster indistinguishable from the next and the occasional FedEx truck trying to make a delivery when nothing has a number or a name. I have to stop twice before finding a dead end and an unmarked steel door that looks like the right one. Even though it's December I'm sweating in my costume, releasing the scent of must and the long-ago deodorant and sweat of a nameless escort or security guard. I breathe through my mouth and hope that no one notices.

After a few rings of the industrial buzzer, I hear the door click unlocked. I push it open and walk in to a fluorescent-lit, low-ceilinged office with gray nubbed carpet. At an old metal desk, a sixty-something receptionist with flame-colored hair, frosted lipstick, and drawn-on eyebrows looks at me in my getup and blinks, then brings her glasses up to her eyes from a rhinestone chain around her neck.

"Can I help you with something?" she asks.

I want to explain it to her but where would I begin? I force a smile and try not to cry.

"I'm here to see Joe?"

I hold the CD player behind me with both hands, as if this will make the whole thing seem more normal.

"In Receiving," she says. "Straight back, make your first right." She crosses her arms across her shelflike bosom and scowls.

I find the department where men mill around boxes

of circuits and electronic parts. It's clearly no bachelor party. Off to the side is a card table with a coffeemaker and boxes of store-bought cookies, and draped across the front of it, a drooping banner reads, "Over the hill!" There is now a film of sweat across my forehead. One of the guys looks at me with a curious grin.

"Joe?" I ask.

No one hears me.

"Excuse me, is there a Joe here?" I ask, raising my voice.

"Uh, I'm Joe," a short guy with gray hair and safety goggles says. "May I help you?"

I pull off my hat and let my tucked up hair fall out.

"Well," I say, "I'm afraid you're under arrest."

A few of the men laugh and clap, pushing a flustered Joe in my direction. I walk toward him with a forced swagger, my hands on my hips.

"Aren't you going to ask me what the charge is?" I ask.

He grimaces, attempting a smile.

"Because," I say, "you are one very sexy birthday boy."

"All right!" someone yells.

"Take it off!" yells another.

They move in, encircling us, and they press Joe down into a plastic chair. He looks pained.

When I press Play, the thumping pop-rhythms of Mariah Carey start in but it takes a few moments for me to start moving—as if I'm in an anxiety dream where I've been pushed out onstage and I can't remember my lines—but then I look at the faces surrounding me, shiny, expectant, and unsure of themselves behind the machismo, and I don't want to disappoint them. Perform, I think, give them what they want.

So I dance, first looking only at Joe in the chair, who doesn't know where to look. I unsnap the first few buttons of my shirt and push my breasts together with my arms at his eye level. The tiniest tease, the smallest step toward a state of undress, elicits whistles of delight. A shoulder, some midriff, even lifting my hair to show my neck is cheered. On each of them I lavish a moment of private eye contact and one-on-one interchange, embarrassing them while at the same time making them want more and more. Kendra was right—I'm glad when the shirt finally comes off. At least I am wearing matching underwear and bra, a new, cream-colored satin and lace combo. I feel less exposed than I would have thought; in fact, I feel protected by an invisible force field separating me from the audience of gaping receiving clerks. And something shifts in me; I am charged. I swing my shirt over my head before letting it fly out into the group. The guy who catches it, one of the younger ones with a sunburned skier's nose, gets his back slapped and hair ruffled as if he were a groom-to-be.

Then I turn back to Joe, whose pleasure is my object. He seems more at ease now and glad to see me. I straddle him on the chair and remove the dime-store handcuffs from the belt loop of my pants. I breathe close to his ear and snap one of the cuffs on his wrist behind the chair—he doesn't resist—and then the other. And while he's cuffed, I sweep my bra-clad breast against his face before I stand and resume my routine, much to the approval of the others. The tight pants have left pink indentations around my waist but no one seems to notice as I peel them down as slowly as I can, bending over to get them past my knees, trying to block out the thought of a bunch of men inches from my butt in the unforgiving light.

When Mariah slips into a slow-jam number, I downshift into what I think is a more sultry act, slithering around the cement-floored workroom in my bra, underwear, and high heels. I take one of the men's hands and he ventures to dance with me, ignoring his mocking coworkers, and for a moment allowing himself to be chosen. I return to Joe, grazing my backside against the back of his head, then spin around and put my foot up on his knee and grind.

Strip-o-grams are supposed to stop here but these guys are stuck in a bland office where I imagine they will be doing the same thing for the rest of their lives. This audience, seemingly so happy and outside themselves, spurs me on. So again I straddle Joe, his wrists still cuffed behind him, kiss his forehead, wink, unhook my bra and slip out of it to the sound of an ovation. Topless, I wrap my bra around Joe's neck and do a brief shimmy before making the rounds from man to man. With a minute to go, I pull down my underwear and step out of them, and in just my heels, raise my arms in a triumphant "ta da!" like a gymnast who just landed a dismount.

When the fervent applause dies down, I stop the CD and scurry for my clothes. In the silence the lights seem brighter and more revealing. The men murmur and pour themselves coffee, with little idea of what to do now. I throw on the big shirt and my underwear.

"Happy Birthday," I say to Joe.

"Thanks. Um. Yeah. Can you unlock me now?" he asks, his voice pleading; sweat bubbles glisten above his lip.

"Oh, sorry," I say, fumbling to find the key.

"Thanks," he says, when his wrists are freed. "That was something."

It is quiet except for the buzz of the lights overhead. I have my bra and pants in one hand, the CD player in the other.

"Oh, wait," one of the guys says, going for his wallet. The others follow suit. Even though I want to run, I don't want to make my exit any more awkward. They hand me all sorts of bills, not even looking at the denominations, just wanting things to get back to normal as soon as possible. I wave with my full hands, and race past the disgusted receptionist to the cold safety of my car. I have $64 in my hand. When my breathing slows, I pull on sweatpants and smoke half a cigarette. It's 3:45.

I drive to Smith's in the Avenues to stroll the aisles, collect myself, and spend my tip. I have the fever-cheek feeling of having hiked all day in a blizzard, the glimmer of having done something dangerous and emerging unscathed. The high lingers.

Spotty snow flurries have begun by the time I pull into the grocery store parking lot. Still reeling, I realize there is something that I have wanted to ask McCallister and I finally have the nerve. I pull over next to the pay phone.

"What are you doing?" I ask.

"Jane? Uh, walking. I just left my shrink's office. What are you doing?"

"Standing in the snow calling you."

"You never call me. Are you okay?"

"Yeah I am, actually."

"You sound weird to me lately."

"I want to ask you something."

"Okay."

"Would you have broken up with me if you hadn't had met Maria?"

"Jane."

A boy in a red Smith's apron pushes a caterpillar of grocery carts past me and waves, glancing quickly at my spiked-heels-and-sweats outfit.

"Hello?" I ask.

"I'm here." McCallister sighs and I know he is running his free hand through his hair. I hear cabs honk in a furious tag-team rhythm. "Why are you asking this? It's been months and months. Does it really matter?"

"Yes, it matters," I say. "It matters to me."

"We would have broken up eventually. You know that. Or we would have split up and gotten back together for years and then where would we have been?"

"So the answer is no?"

"Yes. No is the answer."

"Okay then," I say. "I guess I just needed to know."

"Okay."

"So did Maria paint your walls red yet?"

"No. That's on hold. I mean, the whole thing."

"The whole Maria thing?"

"Yeah. The moving-in part. We're going to wait. See how things go."

The news registers as a shallow sort of win for me.

"I'm sorry, I guess," I say.

"Maybe I'll have to come to Utah and pick up a couple of young wives. Bring them back to my harem."

"I'll keep my eye out for some good candidates," I say.

"Jane, it's not like I don't miss you," he says.

chapter 14

It's a week before Christmas and Ford, Ember, Ralf, and I drive into snow-buried Little Cottonwood Canyon, past the skier-dotted slopes of Solitude, and on to Silver Lake. The one general store out this way is closed for the season, as is the ranger office. Other than a father trying to teach his young daughter how to skate on a cleared square of ice at the far edge, the lake is tranquil and deserted. It's Ford's last day in Salt Lake. The mood is not quite somber, but there is a sense of waiting, of purposely good behavior, of wanting to honor the occasion. We tread lightly in our talk, avoiding the unspoken and unresolved. Our plan is to hike up into the woods to Summer Lake and have a picnic and relish a fragile peace. I'm guessing that with all the gear in our backpacks—sleeping bags, a tarp, a camping stove, bottles of whiskey, wine, and water, blankets, cigarettes, steaks, plates, and utensils—we're not going to make it that far.

Silver Lake has been frozen over for months now, and

it's under two feet of snow. A swollen, dark cloud hovers directly over the peak behind the lake but there are also patches of sun. Ember, who today seems uncharacteristically sober and clear-eyed, points silently toward a pair of moose on the far bank, their hooves buried in snow. The air is so sharp and fresh it hurts at the tail end of a big breath, but so invigorating I can't get enough.

"Hey, do you need some help with that?" I ask Ralf, who's pulling up the rear, his pack clanking with all the bottles. He smiles broadly and shakes his head "no."

"Come on, you guys," Ember calls, leading the way. "The quicker we get there, the quicker we eat."

There's something disorienting about how present Ember is with no drugs; out here in the midst of bare trees and ice and mountains, I feel as if I don't know her at all.

"What's wrong?" Ford asks me.

"Nothing," I say. "It's just cold."

We cross around the southern side of the lake and the incisive high-altitude sun zeroes in and burns my nose and cheeks. About fifty yards back from the lake, a small signpost poking out of the snow marks the beginning of the mile-long trail up into the woods. The sight of it adds twenty pounds to my pack.

"Am I the only one who's tired?" I ask, with rasping breaths. Snow clings to my jeans from my knees on down. My toes are already numb.

"Come on, Jane, you're not ninety," Ember says, motioning me to come along with her scooped hand. "I'm sure Ralf would carry you if you asked." She flashes me a toothy grin, and I give her the finger, which she can't see through my mitten.

"What's that?" Ralf asks, clanking up the rear.

"Nothing," I say.

Ember laughs and launches up the sloping trail with Ford at her heels.

As we climb, the trail cuts through trees and then crosses back over a small open meadow at an easy rise. It is snow-covered and quiet, with only an occasional cry from a hawk and the muted padding of deer hooves scrambling and leaping through the snow in reaction to our appearance. None of us talk but we catch each other's eyes and smile.

When we get to the steep part of the trail, the last quarter mile before Summer Lake, it's a struggle to find purchase on the snow-buried, gnarled tree roots and rocks. I pull myself up, foot by foot, muscling my way, using the young trees and smooth branches for leverage. Ford's outdoorsman skills are an impressive sight; he looks like he belongs, maneuvering with confident grace, completely at ease out here. Unself-conscious among the elements. It makes me want to cry. I have wasted our time together, and now he is going away.

By the time we make it to Summer Lake, my legs are rubbery-weak and I'm gulping for oxygen. Ember unhooks herself from her pack and collapses in a heap right into the snow. Ralf and Ford have fared much better and go straight for the whiskey before even making our little camp. After a silence, Ralf raises the bottle.

"Farewell to our incomparable friend Ford," he says and takes a long swallow from the bottle.

"It's not my funeral," Ford says.

I go for the tarp in my pack and spread it over a flat spot with a view of the small frozen lake through a cluster of pines. Ember has the sleeping bags, which puff up when she pulls them from their cases. Ford expertly sets up the stove while Ralf rights the various bottles to fashion a minibar. Ember reaches for the whiskey and plants it by her side.

With the stove aflame, and the steaks hanging off the sides of the tiny grill, we angle our cocooned bodies like a pinwheel around the fire, with our heads in a center cluster.

"It's not like I'm moving to the moon," Ford says. "Moab's only four and half hours away."

"We'll visit," Ralf says. "Sometime."

Not happy with the turn of the conversation, Ember switches into hostess mode.

"First, down the hatch. Everyone."

I finish my whiskey and my eyes water.

"Okay. Now, Jane, tell us what Ford was like when you met him."

"He skateboarded to class," I say. "And his hair was really long. To hit on girls he would use what he called the ring trick. 'Hey, that's a pretty ring,' he'd say, fondling some poor girl's finger, 'Did your boyfriend give it to you?'"

"It worked. On occasion," Ford says.

"Did it work on you?" Ember asks me.

"No way, I knew his angle."

"Ford, tell us something about Jane," Ember says.

"Oh no," I say.

"Jane, shush," she says.

"We don't have to play this game, do we?" Ralf asks meekly.

Ember ruffles his hair.

"She liked a swimmer dude on my hall," Ford says. "She was aloof. In her flowy skirts and ankle bracelets. Didn't give me the time of day."

"I was thinking more about when you two got hot and heavy," Ember says.

Ford hovers between his loyalties, torn between our history, Ember's dare, and Ralf's sensitivity. Ember casts her expectant eyes toward Ford, and Ralf attempts a laugh to overcome his discomfort.

"It took some time," Ford says. I search out his eyes in the distorting blur above the fire.

"Before you could get in her pants," Ember cuts in.

I glance over to Ralf who has turned a fierce shade of crimson.

"No," Ford says. "It took a while before we became friends. Before it stuck." He is quiet in his sincerity.

I try to smile. I don't ask him if his opinion has changed over the years. I don't ask him if he has ever been disappointed.

"You guys are no fun," Ember says.

Ralf, relieved, snaps back to life and flips the steaks, moving the still-raw ones toward the middle. We pass a bottle. Within minutes, a light dusty snow begins to fall. Ember kisses Ford but it has a sad, loaded quality that makes me feel like a voyeur.

"Hey, Jane, let's take a look at the lake," Ralf says. "While lunch cooks."

We put on our shoes and he holds out his hand to help me up.

Up on a small embankment above the frozen lake, I pull Ralf close with an arm around his middle.

"Hi," I say.

"Hi."

Heavy quiet fills the space between us.

"In 1833, God gave a law of health to Joseph Smith. The Word of Wisdom. Physical and spiritual health by abstaining from tobacco, alcohol, coffee, tea, and illegal drugs. If it turns out to be true, we're all pretty much doomed," he says.

There is another long pause.

"I need to tell you something," I say.

Ralf looks at me.

"I started escorting."

"Oh," he says.

He looks back over his shoulder at the lovebirds then back out at the lake.

"I'm not just on the phone anymore. I go out—"

"I get it. I don't want to know the details."

He eases out of my grip and reaches for a rock, which he proceeds to chuck as far as he can out onto the lake, sending it skidding across the ice.

"I'm sorry I didn't tell you before," I say.

"Hey, it's cool," he says. "It's cool."

I don't know what to say. I feel like burrowing into the nearest foxhole.

"Is it the money?" he asks, turning to me. "Is that it?"

I let out a breath.

"Yeah, partly," I say. "I don't know, Ralf."

His face is mottled and his eyes shift darker. It's as if his whole face is being pulled down as I watch. His eyes droop, his mouth sags. I turn away and look down at small, oblong rabbit tracks that crisscross the top of the snow and head off under the sheltering pines.

"Huh," he says.

"Are you mad?" I ask.

"Mad? That's a weird thing to ask."

I squat and reach for my own rock to throw. The first big snowflakes have begun to fall.

"We're still friends, right?" I ask him lamely. I throw the rock but it gets stuck in a pine branch.

"Of course we are," he says. "I'm fine, Jane. Really. It's no problem."

But I can see from his retreating eyes that he is crushed. Ralf laces his fingers and rests them on his head, then lets his arms fall.

"Tell me something Mormon," I say quietly.

His smile looks bitter now, one side tugging upward without the strength to pull up the other side.

"How about we try to crack the ice with this one?" Ralf kicks a large chunk of granite submerged in snow and frozen earth. "What do you say? Do you think I can do it?"

I smile and Ralf crouches down to wrench it free. He pulls up on the rock, discarding his gloves for a better grip, his knuckles white from strain. Like a weight lifter, he cleans-and-jerks it first to shoulder level, then above his head. With a few steps, he hurls it out onto the iced-over lake, where it lands with a deadened thwack. I hear a long, chills-inducing squeak and pop before I see the crack shoot toward us from where the boulder hit. It tracks us all the way to the shore.

"How about that," he says.

*

"Hi Mom."

"Hi honey. Sorry I haven't called you back. I'm making a coffee cake for brunch tomorrow at the Walters. But I can't seem to find—oh there it is."

"Pecan or blueberry?"

"Blueberry. Karen claims to be allergic to nuts."

A dish clatters.

"I have some bad news," I say.

"Is everything okay? What's wrong?"

"Nothing's wrong, don't worry. But I don't think I can make it home for Christmas."

"What? Oh no, Jane, really? Why not? Your sister's arriving tomorrow. The tree's already up."

"I know, I'm sorry. It's just a crazy season at work. I thought I'd be able to swing it but it's not looking too promising."

Frost has taken up on the corners of the windows, glittering in the light from streetlamp.

"I just don't understand a job that won't let you go home for Christmas."

"I think it will slow down in the new year. I'm sorry, Mom."

She sighs. "It's the first Christmas we won't all be together."

I squeeze my eyes shut. "I know."

"I'd let you say hello to your father but he's already asleep," she says.

I hear her open a cupboard door.

"Janie, are you okay? You're so quiet."

"Yeah. I'm fine."

"Well, all right, if you say so. Oh shoot, I knew I should have gotten more butter. Do you think I can substitute olive oil for some of it?"

chapter 15

Nikyla, fresh from her manager shift at the mall, is in a suit and her black hair is pulled neatly in a low ponytail. Despite my ten-year age advantage, I feel younger than she is as I settle next to her on the couch.

"How long has it been for you here?" I ask.

"Eight and a half months. Three and a half months to go," she says.

"So exact."

"That's the plan."

"Do you ever think about the girls that quit? Like do you wonder what happens to them, or think you pass them in the street? They just seem to drop off the radar when they leave."

"I like to think they went on to do what they wanted. In a play on Broadway, maybe, or living in Paris, or married with two kids." She smiles. "And if they can do it, so can I."

Mohammed wanders in from the back, working out

the Christmas schedule on the side of an envelope.

"Remember the one that started right after Thanksgiving. Pamela?" I ask. "I wonder about her. I wonder if her boyfriend came back or if she moved to Kansas or if she got a job in a doctor's office. Who knows? She could be sailing around the world."

"She's working over at Baby Dolls," Nikyla says.

"No way," I say.

"It is the truth," Mohammed chimes in.

"She was so devastated that first time she went out. She said she couldn't do it anymore," I say.

"You give these girls too much credit," he says.

"Watch it. I'm one of 'these girls,'" I say.

Nikyla smiles.

"So you are." Mohammed rubs his chin.

"She looks better," Nikyla says. "Pamela. Or whatever her real name is. I ran into her at the mall a couple weeks ago. She didn't know I worked there."

Mohammed looks down at the empty holiday schedule.

"I can work Christmas Eve and Christmas," I say.

"You are volunteering?" he asks. "This is very peculiar." He walks out of the office shaking his head.

Nikyla pats my knee.

"I have to go. One-year anniversary tonight. When Jezebel gets here will you tell her to call me on my cell?"

A half hour later Jezebel comes in before going downtown to the Hyatt to meet her date, a semi-regular who comes into town every couple months and only wants blonds. It's the first I've seen her since her arrest. She's in a tame getup for her—black pants and tank top—beneath her puffy white coat.

"Where's Albee?" I ask.

"My mom's got him. I waited until she was drunk so I knew she'd say yes," she says, slumping down into the couch. "You didn't tell Mohammed, did you?" she asks.

"Course not," I say.

Jezebel dangles her shoe on her sloppily painted pink toe and scowls.

"What's wrong?"

"I was sort of dating this guy, hooking up, whatever. Jared. Really cute. But he hasn't called in, like, four days."

"What happened?" I ask.

She lowers her head and looks up at me.

"What do you think?"

"You told him?" I ask.

"I didn't think it would be a big deal. He was talking about how he dated a stripper once and he thought it was hot, so I told him."

Sunk in between the couch cushions and buried within the down fluff of her jacket, she looks swallowed up.

"You're just a kid, you know," I say. "One day this will all just be some crazy thing you did when you were young. A shocking little story you'll like to tell."

She snorts and takes an old issue of *Vogue* from the coffee table and stuffs it into her bag.

"Roxanne, you need to stop watching so much *Oprah*," she says, getting up. "Sometimes things just suck and there's no explanation that makes it better. I'll call when I get there."

When the door closes behind her, another flurry of brown pine needles blankets the carpet. I take the dead wreath down and set it outside the door. I'm frustrated by my inability to cheer Jezebel up. The colored lights on the Christmas tree blink on and off, and since I don't know how to make them stop, I unplug the whole thing. To combat my heavy head, I turn on all the lights, straighten the cushions, crack the window to clear out some of the parched air, empty the ashtray, and wipe the crumbs from the table. But with the lights on, it looks sad and naked so I turn them all off again just in time to answer the phone, put McCallister on hold, and send Mimi on a date to the Marriott up near the university.

"Hi," I say, clicking back over to McCallister.

"What did that guy want?"

"'Oriental.' Fortunately I had Mimi available."

"Yeah," he says. "How late are you working?"

"Till ten."

"So how's it going?"

"McCallister, are you trying to work up to something? No need to beat around the bush."

"Okay, then, two things. One, I'm worried about you. You seem like you're hiding something and you still seem depressed."

"You're the one who seems depressed," I say.

"Jane, please. The other is Maria's not moving in because she found out how often I talk to you."

"I figured Maria was going to find out eventually and then we'd have the we-can't-talk-anymore-because-it-makes-her-uncomfortable talk. Is that what this is?"

"It's hardly that simple."

"Does that mean you're not going to call me anymore?" My anger is thinly disguised.

"Let's talk about the other issue first," he says.

"Issue?"

"What is it with you? What's going on? Have you become a drug addict or something? Are you going to put stones in your pockets and walk into the Great Salt Lake?"

"Maybe it's just that I'm living a new life and trying to distance myself from the old. Maybe I've met someone."

"Is that true?" he asks.

"No. But it could be. Look, nothing's wrong. I'm fine."

"Are you with Ford?"

"Figures you'd say that. Jesus. Ford is leaving for Moab tomorrow, so no. Ember's staying here with me."

"That makes me feel a lot better."

"You broke up with me, remember?"

"You're my friend. I want you to be happy."

"You want me to be happy so you can feel less guilty."

"Jane."

"What."

"I can't have this conversation over the phone."

"What conversation is that?"

"This. Everything. Us."

"Us?"

"I'm coming to see you," he says.

"I'm holding my breath."

"In a week."

"You're not invited." Two other lines ring but I let them go.

"I don't need to be invited. I need to work this out face-to-face."

"You need to work this out? You don't get to pick. You don't always get your way, McCallister. This is your problem, not mine. There's nothing to work out. You don't want to talk anymore? Fine. Don't call me. It's that simple. Have a great life with Maria. I'm giving you my blessing. Is that what you're looking for? I'm not pining over you. I'm not waiting for you to come to your senses. I've moved on."

"Did Ford help you with that impassioned speech?"

The red lights of the other lines have stopped flashing on the phone.

"Enough. Please. I have to go."

"Because your madame job is so important to you now?"

"Fuck you. I'm hanging up now."

"I'll see you soon," he says.

"No you won't. I'm telling you not to."

I slam the phone down.

*

When my shift ends at ten, I go to my car only to find Ford leaning against it.

"Hey," I say.

I collapse a bit in his hug.

"What's wrong?" he asks, his chin on my head.

"Ralf hates my guts, McCallister is threatening to come here, and you're leaving tomorrow. Where should I start?"

"I'm leaving tonight," he says. "I'm on my way."

I pull away to look at him in the alley lamplight.

"The longer I wait, the worse it'll be," he says. "No use tacking on another night of trying to prepare to say good-bye. Ember acts like it's some sort of betrayal that I'm going but she's the one who's changing the plans."

"What's going to happen now with you guys?"

"I don't know. We'll talk. We'll visit a couple days here and there. She'll find someone new. Move on. Leave without saying good-bye."

"That's bleak."

"I'm not saying anything you don't already know," he says.

"Then why leave?"

"Because I don't belong here," he says. "The job's over. I feel stuck. And I've always known it was up to her."

I hold his palms to my cheeks.

"So what's this about McCallister?" he asks.

I shake my head. "I forbade him but he says he's coming to Salt Lake."

"I knew that guy would realize he'd made a mistake. Do you want my two cents? You're better without him."

"I know."

"At least don't do anything dumb like sleep with him."

"Don't worry. He's practically married," I say.

"Not if he's coming here to see you," he says.

I shrug, because I have nothing else to say.

"If things get rough up here, you know you can come down to me. You'll always have a place in the trailer," Ford says.

"Thanks."

"And Jane?"

"Yeah?"

"Don't follow her too closely."

I want him to clarify, but I have enough of a sense of what he means and it looks too painful for him to continue.

"I love you, kid," I say.

"I love you too," he says.

I kiss his cold, chapped lips and hang on, longer than I should, until he gently pulls free. I walk him to his truck, already loaded up with what little he brought to Salt Lake, and I touch the window before my sweet-souled fair-haired friend drives away.

"Hey Roxanne!" Kendra calls from the door of the office. "Want to go see Cully?"

I've sent girls to Cully before. He has a strong East Texas twang and he likes to get peed on.

"What the hell," I say.

*

I've never peed on anyone before. On what part of him do I pee? Do I do it in the bathtub? In the bed?

Cully actually says "Howdy" when he opens the door. He's tall and beanpole skinny, with the expected mustache, and he's clad in a white T-shirt and tight Wranglers. Although he seems easygoing, he shows up on some of the girls' "will not see" lists on account of his golden shower proclivity as well as for a propensity for getting aggressive. Tonight I feel like I can handle whatever he throws my way because all I want to do is forget everything else.

"Hello," I say, "I'm Roxanne."

"Rox-anne," he sings in his best Sting imitation. "Welcome. Make yourself at home."

We're at the Crystal Inn downtown, on the twenty-fifth floor overlooking Temple Square. The room, in shades of sea foam and mauve, has an early-eighties, smooth-cornered feel to it. Cully clicks off the hockey game and dives onto the bed.

"Money's on the TV there," he says.

After I call in, Cully says he's going to take a shower and that I should relax. I step out of my shoes and coat and curl up on the bed in my jeans. He sings Garth Brooks in the shower and I switch on the TV and turn to a cooking show on PBS.

I imagine Ford in his truck, just past Provo around Spanish Fork, with Johnny Cash on the tape deck, thinking about the last month. I wonder how he will remember it, how he will give it shape and meaning, how Ember will become understandable in memory in a way she wasn't in person. I feel his absence and I feel relief. With Ford gone, I don't have to explain what I'm doing. I don't have to have a good reason.

"Hey, Roxy baby," Cully sings, dancing out of the bathroom with a towel around his waist. His hair is slicked back, and water drips from his mustache. A puckered diagonal scar on his abdomen, I assume from an appendectomy, and a blurry blue tattoo on his bicep are his distinguishing marks.

"Hey there, Cully," I say, crossing my legs Indian-style.

"Want to dance, lovely lady?" he asks, swinging his narrow hips from side to side.

I have to laugh. He takes me by the hands with surprising force and pulls me across the bed. When I'm on my feet in front of him, he unzips my sweatshirt in one quick pull and puts his hands around my waist, swaying to nonexistent music.

"Slow down there," I say, losing my balance.

"Don't worry, I've got you," he says. He slides off my sweatshirt and slips his hands under my shirt. "Want a pick-me-up? A kick of speed might loosen you up."

"No, thanks," I say, "but some music would be nice."

He rolls his eyes but lets me go turn on the radio, which is playing the end of an old Pearl Jam song. When I turn back, he's let the towel drop and his hand is on his semi-erect penis.

"Come back here, you," he says. "Let's have ourselves some fun."

I walk toward him and he reaches out and yanks me to him by my belt loops.

"Off with these," he says, going right for my zipper.

I coyly push him away and get out of my jeans on my own, and before he asks, I take off my shirt.

"Whoo!" he cheers, dancing to Britney Spears. "Come on, Roxanne, don't you want just a taste? One little bump?"

And then I think, why not? Why not shut off my mind for a little while.

I follow him into the bathroom, where he cuts clumped white powder on the back of the toilet. With a pocketknife, he takes a small pile up each nostril. He hands me the knife and I do the same, the chemical drip in my throat promising an altered state I long for. I feel it almost immediately in my heart and I reach up and kiss Cully on the cheek.

"Thanks, darlin'," he says.

He starts to lead me by the hand but then picks me up, as if carrying me over the threshold, with one arm hooked under my knees and one around my back, and sets me on the bed. The drugs have shrouded me in a layer of remove. I close my eyes and feel his body on mine, his lips on my neck, his hands seeking out mine. He smells like Speed Stick and tobacco. I like the breathless feeling of all his weight on me. I have nothing to do but be here as a body. Cully gets his hands underneath my butt and flips me over on top of him. When I open my eyes, I'm dizzy. I feel his erect penis against my stomach.

"Yeah," he says. "Yeah, come on. Give it to me."

His hands are pressed on my thighs as I kneel above him. For a moment, I feel totally lost. No memory, no fear, no awareness. An empty vessel. He groans as he masturbates and the sound of his voice snaps me back.

I have pee fright and I have to think of waterfalls to get it going as he begs me to do it now, do it now.

"I want to feel it on me," he says.

I close my eyes and feel the odd freedom of letting go right here. My aim is not great but I adjust so the urine stream hits right on his frantic hand, and he ejaculates as if on command.

"Shit, yeah," he says, flopping into a spread eagle position and closing his eyes.

I move off the wet bed and reach for my jeans.

"Roxanne, come here baby," he says. He slaps my butt hard. "Yeah. Real nice. Go in the front pocket of my pants over there. There's a little something for you."

It's a hundred dollars.

"Thanks," I say.

I haven't been called out yet, but the date is all over.

"Drive safe," Cully says, lighting a cigarette and turning the hockey game back on.

When the door shuts, I hear him yelling at the TV. I stand in the hall and listen as Cully claps and hoots. It makes me smile that he was pleased with my performance. My heart jumps about and I feel warm and riled up from the drugs and from the afterglow of having had a momentary, crystalline sense of purpose.

I jog to the elevator.

chapter 16

With Ford gone, Ember moves from the makeshift living room sleeping area into my room, right into my bed. She comes in early the next morning—she's been out all night—and snuggles against me in her clothes. I feel sleepy happiness with her beside me. In a sense I've gotten what I've been after for weeks, though I know it's a fleeting arrangement. We sleep until eleven, content to laze about until noon, getting sweaty under the covers.

"My breath could kill someone," she says, rolling over.

Ember knows that I know she wasn't with Ford and she wasn't here, but I don't ask her where she's been.

"I had to pee on someone last night," I say.

"No way! I haven't even done that yet. Oh remind me, I have some money for you."

"Okay," I say. "Thanks." Her contributions to the household are spotty but I take what I can get.

"Did you see Ford before he left?" she asks.

"Yeah. He came by the office."

"Do you think I'm a bad person for not going with him?"

"As if I'm in any position to judge anyone," I say.

"It's not the right thing for me to follow him down there. It would make me resent him eventually," she says. "He's way too good to be subjected to that."

"Well, if it matters, I'm glad you stayed," I say. I want to sink down into right here forever.

Ember hooks her fingers into mine.

"Of course it matters," she says.

"So what now?" I ask, half-hoping she'll decide everything for me, take away the uncertainty and fear of what I'm supposed to do next.

Ember shrugs and hooks her leg onto mine.

"Jane?"

"Yeah?"

"Has there been anyone since McCallister?"

"Nah."

"Don't you miss it?"

I think about sex and the first things that come to mind are peeing and hockey.

"Not really," I say. "In an abstract way, I guess. The longer it's been, the more remote it seems. I miss the first skin-to-skin contact under the covers. Getting hugged from behind. Having a neck to kiss. Mostly, I think I miss being part of something everyone else isn't in on."

"That makes me sad," Ember says. "When I'm alone I miss sex almost immediately. The leading-up-to-it part and the sex itself. That's when I'm okay. But the minute it's over and he pulls away, the clock starts ticking and it won't be long until I start feeling lost, like I might float away."

"Is that true?" I ask.

"Well, not really float away, but yeah."

"Even with Ford?"

"Especially with Ford because he thinks it's all something it's not. And I'm reminded of that every time."

Ember picks at lint on the comforter. "But you're doing it again. You always masterfully deflect my prying. So why are you here anyway?"

"Here?"

"Here. Utah. This bed."

My face burns.

"There's no shame in hiding out, if that's it. That's pretty much my game. Flee from one haven to the next, as long as it protects or distracts me. Survive the time. Don't think that I'm too far gone to notice the pattern." She nudges me with her shoulder. "What are you hiding from?"

I put a pillow over my face but Ember pulls it away and pokes me in the arm.

"I don't think of it as hiding," I say. "More like removing myself so I can do things differently. Not starting over but consciously choosing something for a change. Not just going along with circumstance."

"That sounds good but I have a feeling that this is about McCallister," she says.

"Now you sound like him. No. That's over."

"When is anything with a man ever over?"

"I want it to be."

"Okay, okay. Then what about Ford?"

"What about him?"

"Oh come on. You two are both a little in love with each other."

She interrupts my sputtering protest with a laugh.

"I think it's sweet," she says.

I sit up.

"That's not it. Really," I say.

"Just think of me now and again when you're growing old together."

The phone rings until the machine clicks on.

"Um, Shena, it's noon and you're on call. Hello? Are you there?"

"Shit," Ember says, oozing out of bed.

She cuts two lines of cocaine on the bedside table. The dreamy morning evaporates while Kendra rattles on.

"Okay already," Ember says, snorting up one and then the other with a well-used straw. She keeps on her outfit from the night before, still reeking of smoke, pulls her hair into a lopsided ponytail and quickly sniffs her armpits. Gargling a mouthful of mouthwash, she grabs her keys and she's out the door, leaving it open behind her.

*

Nikyla and Jezebel are on the couch, flipping through

a Delia's catalog.

"This is a good look for you, Rox," Nikyla says holding up the catalog.

"That skirt's so short," I say. "Maybe if I were ten years younger."

"You always say that but we're all just girls here. Age doesn't mean anything," Jezebel says. She lies down on Nikyla's lap and hangs her legs over the side of the couch with Albee asleep on her stomach.

"Have you talked to that guy you were dating?" I ask.

Jezebel shakes her head "no."

"Listen," Nikyla says. "He's not worth your time. The right one will love you no matter what."

Jezebel shrugs, unconvinced, and points to some skater pants.

"Yeah, those are cute," Nikyla says. "You can get some like it at the store. Use my discount."

"Hey, Roxanne. Did you hear what happened to Miranda last night?" Jezebel asks, readjusting the puppy.

"She was almost raped," Nikyla says.

"What?" I'm stunned by the revelation and by their prioritizing it behind cute pants.

"She ran out with only her purse. Her arms and legs had all these bruises," Jezebel says. "The dickhead even called out after her that she forgot her clothes."

Her nonchalance is forced. I know this reminder of what could happen brings our vulnerability into stark relief.

"Is she okay?" I ask.

Nikyla looks up from the catalog at the blinds-shaded window.

"She called in a couple hours after she got home but no one's seen her since. She hasn't come in," Jezebel says, trying hard to play down the incident so she'll be able to face another date.

"I talked to her," Nikyla says. "She said she's leaving. Going to Idaho to her parents'. She doesn't sound that good."

"Was he arrested?"

"Yeah, right," Jezebel says, sitting up.

"Come on, Rox, even you're not that naïve," Nikyla says with uncharacteristic edge. "It's not like she didn't take the money."

"What does Mohammed say?"

Both girls just look at me. I feel queasy.

Jezebel says in a mocking Arabic accent, "Just put him on the 86ed list and don't send anyone to see him. It's over. No one gets hurt."

Kendra is murmuring in her best phone sex voice back at the desk.

"Jezebel," Kendra says, "Don Steele at the Marriott."

"Score," Jezebel says. "That means presents."

I feel like shaking them until they break and their fear tumbles out.

"Oh, I forgot to tell you. Josh got the promotion. He's manager now," Nikyla says, examining her face in a compact.

"You know what that means," Jezebel says.

Nikyla makes a rocking cradle with her arms.

"Really?" I ask.

"As soon as possible," Nikyla says.

I force a smile. But I feel the need to flee.

*

It's four o'clock as I drive west out of town toward Wendover. The news of the assault and of Nikyla's impending pregnancy has left me feeling raw. All I can stomach is driving. A trip through the expansive, moon-like Bonneville Salt Flats seems the only palatable option. The sun is already orange and sinking ahead. To my right, the Morton Salt factory perched on the edge of the lake is idle and vacant.

I never would have admitted it at the time but I thought McCallister and I were going to get married. It was not something I actively hoped for. I had just assumed. We were different than other people. We were weird. We were a team. I couldn't imagine anyone else understanding me the way I thought he did. I thought that as long as McCallister needed me enough, I'd win by default.

When we had been together only two months—still feeling blithe and unstoppable—I got pregnant. McCallister was coolheaded about it while I was terrified. He said all the right things: the timing is wrong, we're not ready, it's a practical decision, we'll have plenty of time, we'll get through this. He said all those abstract niceties that made me feel better on the surface, but he shied away from the messy undertow. I let him.

He went with me to the clinic, he paid for it, he held my hair when I threw up into a paper bag in the cab on the way home, he took care of me afterward and brought me chocolate and movies and maxi pads for the endless flow of blood. He asked me how I was but I knew he didn't want to hear that I hurt, that I was seized by cramps, that I resented him, that I felt a lack.

"I'm fine," I said again and again, and seeing as we didn't know each other well and that he was trying his best, I let it go at that. And so did he. In the days, weeks, months that followed, I stowed the memory, and every scrap that clung to it, in a crevice of my head, forcing my mind to imagine a blank page whenever I would think of it, congratulating myself when the stretches between remembrances grew further apart.

We never talked about it. Sometimes I wonder if he's forgotten. Or maybe it's something he could never quite get over. At least with Maria he has a clean slate.

The salt flats are eerily white and sere, tinged pink by the setting sun. Smooth planes of water surround the craggy rock formations to the north, and the resulting reflections make them look like floating meteors. The thought passes through my head that if I stay on I-80, I'd end up in San Francisco, which has a certain appeal. But I have to pee and I haven't eaten all day and I'm not that deluded as to try running away again.

So I exit. Wendover is half in Utah, half in Nevada, and the Utah side is a meager strip of trailers, a bodega, a gas station, a Mormon church, and little else. The state taxes are higher, so there's no incentive to live on this side of the line except to uphold some moral obligation to the church.

The Nevada Wendover is a small gambling oasis taunting and tempting Utahns to come over for a spell, a brightly lit miniature Oz emerging from the desert over-look. Giant Wendover Will, a neon, pointing cowboy with a cigarette in his mouth, marks the Stateline Casino, and a "This Is the Place" sign mocks its counterpoint back in Salt Lake.

The rodeo is in town and it looks as if I've wandered onto a western movie set. Every man I see has a cowboy hat on, and every woman has a chambray shirt tucked into tight jeans. I slip into the clanging sea of the casino, where I go unnoticed against a backdrop of blinking lights, slot machine bells, and the sound of coins falling into metal trays. No clocks, no visible exits, no windows, just the smell of stale smoke, the metallic tang of money, and the itch to win. I find a five-dollar blackjack table and an empty stool next to a young guy with a florid face and a black Stetson. The knuckles of his hand tapping the table for a hit are scabbed and cracked. He nods when I sit and turns his attention back to the dealer.

When the hand is done, the dealer (Sheila, Fresno,

CA) busts. She's thirty-five or so, with frosted hair, and she's pudgy but attractive, with slender hands and rich brown eyes. I flatten three twenties in front of me on the table. She displays the money for a hidden camera in the ceiling before stuffing it into the slot and expertly clicking and stacking chips. An older couple on the end thank her, wish her a Merry Christmas, and leave the table.

It's just the cowboy and I. Sheila the dealer points the yellow plastic card at me to cut. I want her to like me. I cut the deck, and right off bet a dollar tip for her alongside my own hand. I split eights against her seven showing. The cowboy holds at eighteen. He wins, I win both hands, and Sheila doubles her tip. She thanks me with a slight smile. I actually give the cowboy a high five. He says his name is Boyd. My whiskey arrives just as a new round begins and I feel lucky and energized and anonymous, one with these two, giving an evil eye to a woman in a sequined top who considers joining our group.

But by the time my third drink arrives, Sheila is on a winning streak and I'm down $150, and Boyd now scowls and bites his nails. I like to think we share at the moment one simple desire: to be dealt good cards. When a new dealer comes to take over for Sheila, Boyd looks forlorn, abandoned, as if she owed it to us to stay and help dig us out.

"Come on," he says to her. "Just a few more hands?"

The spell has been broken. Now down $200, it seems a steeper climb back up with mustached, tan Marty, Elko, NV, dealing the cards.

"Shit," Boyd says, lifting his hat and replacing it on his head.

"Here for the rodeo?" I ask.

"Yeah. Going back to Rock Springs for Christmas then I compete here again. I'm a bull rider."

"Wow," I say.

I finally win a hand.

"How 'bout y'all?" Boyd asks.

"I've never ridden a bull," I say.

This makes him chuckle.

"Shit!" he yells when he hits a sixteen with a queen. Boyd looks barely older than twenty.

The dealer's hands are smooth and lotion-shiny. His nails are buffed. The hungry way Boyd and I watch those hands makes me think that a table dealer is not so different from an escort. Offering the hope of redemption, for a price. And even though we know better, we're tempted again and again by the new promise, just this once, just one more, maybe this time. Knowledge that a game is fixed doesn't curb the urge to play.

I lose another three hands and I'm down a month's rent. The dealer flicks his eyes to me as if in warning but I'm close to very drunk and not far, I think, from winning it all back. Boyd brazenly hits a seventeen against the dealer's king and I follow suit, doubling down on a nine, matching my reckless hundred-dollar bet. With an unlikely four of clubs, Boyd hits big with twenty-one and he pumps his fists in the air. For me, eighteen and twenty beats Marty's seventeen and Boyd catches me in a clumsy hug.

"Hot damn," he says as the dealer counts out stacks of chips for both of us. We slide a few back in his direction as a tip. "What do you say? Quit on this high note in all our glory?" he asks me.

I'm still down $300 but I'm intrigued by Boyd's youthful exuberance. He tips his hat back and rubs his hands on his denim-sheathed thighs.

"Bets folks?" the dealer asks.

"I'm out," I say.

"Me too." Boyd says. "Where to?" he asks with an eager smile.

"Maybe some air," I say, sliding off the stool.

I pick up my coat from the floor and feeling unsteady on my feet, I have to grab onto the edge of the table. Boyd's hand and forearm—over-developed, I assume, from hanging onto a bull for his life—guide me to an exit I wouldn't begin to be able to find on my own.

It's late, the night before Christmas Eve, and outside the carnival-like casino it's quiet and dry-cold as only the high-desert winter can be. I can't see stars because of the lights but I imagine that over the salt flats they are dense and consoling, making the big sky seem less of an unfathomable abyss.

"Shit, it's nippy," Boyd says.

"Yeah." I lean against a wall to stop the spins. I want to lie down with my face against the frozen sidewalk.

"I won two hundred bucks," he says. "A Christmas bonus."

I don't want him to talk. I want him to pick me up and carry me somewhere so I can sleep.

"I watched them filming *Touched by an Angel* yesterday over there in Salt Lake City. It was pretty neat. Saw that Roma Downey and the other one, the black woman with the white stripe in her hair. You watch that show?"

I shake my head with my eyes closed.

"I like it sometimes," he says. "So what do you like to watch?"

His attempt at small talk is endearing but I don't have the energy.

"Where're you staying?" I ask.

He turns away and coughs.

"Uh, the Best Western. Down a ways."

"How old are you?" I ask.

"Twenty-five."

I know he's lying but I think it's to make me feel better.

"You're sweet," I say.

"My dad's in the room. He's taking me back to Wyoming tomorrow. He's there. He's asleep." Boyd snaps his fingers.

"Oh," I say, stifling a laugh.

"What about you?"

"Salt Lake City," I say, knowing a hundred miles is not an option.

He takes off his hat, looks at it, and puts it back on.

"I have a good idea," he says.

His large calloused hand takes mine and pulls me back into Stateline, back into the jarring blur. I am so relieved to be led. I watch my feet against the red carpet, bump into people without looking up. Boyd steers us to the motel end of the casino and pays for a room with his winnings.

He's gentle, as if I am a wounded bird. He takes off my coat and my sneakers, eases me down on the bed in the dark room. I close my eyes and feel his fingers fumble with the button fly of my jeans. He pulls down the covers and lifts me up over them. I open my eyes and smile so he doesn't think I've passed out and he touches my cheek. He continues with the rest of my clothes, and I give myself over to the kindness in his hands. It's the first time I have been with someone since McCallister and I fight the instinctive shift into a needing-to-please mode. After a quick strip of his own clothes and the crinkle of a retrieved condom, I feel his warm body beside me, his rough hand softly running along my arm.

Boyd kisses me and I kiss him back without opening my eyes and without words. I pull him close and rock him so he rolls on top of me; I want his weight and his warmth and his skin to press me through to the bottom of the bed. His body is taut and new, and I feel his gratitude, as if he can't believe his good fortune. I let him give. He moves his hands lovingly over my breasts, where he lays his head for a moment like a baby against his mother.

"I don't even know your name," he whispers.

I open my eyes, jarred by the unfamiliar face in the dark. "Jane," I say.

"Jane," he says. "I'm Boyd."

I close my eyes again. "I know."

Boyd moves down to kiss my stomach. I stay motionless and focus on the warm track his touch leaves on my skin. I sense his hesitation in the face of my silent stillness—he is waiting, I know, for a sign. But I'm thankful he doesn't say anything. I don't want to hear his voice or decipher words. I float, moored only by the slippery body of the young cowboy on top of me. I match my breathing to his, faster, shallower, urgent. I imagine myself melting slowly into the bed like hot, poured honey.

*

"Can I tell you something?" Boyd asks, after I have settled in on my side of the bed, welcoming sleep.

"That's the first time I've done it in a bed," he says. "It's usually a car or something. This was real nice."

I turn to his cherubic face.

"Thanks, Boyd," I says. "It was real nice."

"Yeah?" he asks brightly.

"Yeah," I say.

"'Night," he says, smiling.

*

At dawn, I wake to the sound of cowboy boots on the landing outside the door as the other rodeo guests head home for Christmas Eve. I sneak back into my clothes and I'm out the door as Boyd slumbers in innocence. My head thuds behind my eyes in the light and my mouth feels sucked dry with a foul aftertaste. I burn it away with industrial coffee from the gas station, but instead of going to my car, I decide to try and win back what I lost.

Parrot Bay, near the end of the strip, is well past its prime. The cocktail waitresses are middle-aged and the local clientele burned-out. It's empty, save for a couple of gray-haired women in white gloves, now coin-dirty, feeding nickels into slot machines, and a few woolly sorts slumped over the bar. I find the one blackjack table open for business and get to work.

But I have no connection with the dealer, a brusque older man without a name tag who rarely looks at me and carries on a conversation with the bored-looking pit boss. I lose fast. With careless bets and rotten luck, the two hundred I won back goes in ten minutes and I'm down five hundred dollars. The thought of being short on rent makes me feel nauseated, as does the cigarette I smoke down on an empty stomach. I leave the table without a good-bye to the uncharitable dealer and steel myself for the blinding morning glare outside.

But then near the exit I spy a phone.

"Hello?" McCallister says quietly.

"Why are you talking so quietly?"

"Hold on a second." There are fumbling sounds, then that of a door closing. "Maria's asleep. What time is it out there?"

"I don't know. Morning sometime."

"It's not even seven yet your time. You must be really excited for Christmas Eve."

"I can't wait."

"So what's going on?"

"Remember that time we drove to Atlantic City?"

"A total disaster," he says.

"Well, I'm in Wendover. I lost a bit," I say.

"Jane, go home. Please? Just don't do anything until I get there."

"No. Listen. Please, please don't come here. That's why I'm calling. I don't want to see you. I want to live my life, everything, by myself."

There is a pause. I'm not sure I've ever heard him so quiet.

"Merry Christmas," I say, and hang up.

I speed through the limitless arid and empty salt flats toward home.

chapter 17

When I arrive home, my apartment is quiet, but then Ember staggers into the living room in the same clothes she's been wearing for days, her hair stringy around her face.

"Where have you been?" she asks. There is a twinge of sharpness in her voice. "I waited up for you last night."

"What's wrong?"

"Nothing," she says, slumping down into the couch. "I just thought you'd be here."

She wipes her nose on her sleeve and starts to wag her bare foot—surprisingly small and girlish—with manic speed. "I have to tell you something you're not going to like."

"What is it?"

"I'm going to Moab."

"But I thought—"

"Just for a few days. For Christmas." Ember picks at a scab on her hand with such irritation and hostility that I'm guessing she must be out of drugs.

"Oh," I say, trying not to show how let down I feel,

trying to play down the fact that Ember has chosen to be with Ford over me. "I guess that'll be nice for you guys."

"You can come if you want," she says.

"I have to work," I say, sounding more pouty than I want to. "But thanks."

"Okay. Well, I'm going to head out. You sure you don't want to come?" she asks.

I nod, letting the feeling of abandonment settle in my chest.

*

It's bright and unseasonably warm out, but on the day before Christmas in Salt Lake City, everything is closed. The broad streets are empty of traffic, and despite the cheery sun, it feels deserted and lonely. Even Smith's is closed, barring me from its aisles of refuge. The only place I find open is the 7-Eleven, where I buy Diet Coke, two bruised bananas, brownie mix, milk, corn flakes, and a sorry-looking Golden Delicious apple for my Christmas Eve feast.

"It looks like we're the only ones out and about today," I say to the clerk, a burly Samoan missing his front bottom teeth.

"$11.60," he says.

When I'm back at home, my mom calls but I let the answering machine take it. I eat a bowl of cereal, make the brownies, and eat half the batch while watching a biography of Jesus on TV. McCallister is at his parents' house up the Hudson with Maria, Ember is on her way to be with Ford, Boyd the young cowboy is home by now with his family in Wyoming, and in Cleveland, I imagine my mom is hanging the last of the antique ornaments while my sister complains about how selfish I am for not coming home and my dad tunes them out with his third Scotch. I try to feel freedom in my invisibility. With Christmas music on the radio I bathe, lying motionless in the water until my fingers and toes are withered into sunken crevices and I've begun to sweat. I can survive alone. I just wish there were a way to dull the ache.

At seven o'clock I get a call from Marisa, who has a date for me. It's the taxidermist. I laugh when she tells me. I am relieved to have an assignment on Christmas Eve, rescued from my brooding by a mission to make back the rent money I lost in Wendover. From the look of what I put on—long black velvet skirt, gray silk blouse, demure, rose-colored lipstick—and my upswept hair, one might assume I am on my way to Christmas mass, if not for the stiletto pumps that look like two shiny black weapons in the icy porch light.

State Street is all lit up with no one to see it but me. Blinking Santas and snowmen adorn every car dealership and fast-food restaurant. There's even a huge green plastic wreath on the front door of American Bush. I belt out "White Christmas" and "Jingle Bell Rock" and "Silent Night." I dance in my seat to the jaunty tempo of Mannheim Steamroller's "Joy to the World" as I drive south past West Jordan, trying to coerce my spirits into staying aloft. I pass Lehi, Pleasant Grove, and the "happy valley" of Provo. But the clusters of lights and buildings begin to peter out after Payson and I have to work harder at staying upbeat. Finally I reach Santaquin and I know I can't be that far.

The weather-beaten Utah map I bought on my drive west has a hole in its corner fold where Nephi should be, so with Marisa's help I scratched out some directions to Ephraim's on the edge of a Chinese take-out menu. Although I've never been to Nephi, I'm not too worried about getting lost in a town with the same population as my high school.

Nephi, Ralf once told me, was founded by two LDS leaders who were instructed by church higher-ups in the mid-nineteenth century to lay out a town at the mouth of Salt Creek Canyon. Like most of Juab County, it's rural and almost entirely Mormon, rumored to be rife with fundamentalist polygamists. A large percentage of the residents are direct descendents of the city's founders. I wish it were daylight so I could get a glimpse of Mount Nebo as I drive south into town, if only for some reassurance that the world has not slid away.

Main Street is desolate and it looks like a Depression-era dust bowl holdout. There is one flickering streetlight and the windows of the small shops are dark. I expect tumbleweeds to roll by. My directions point me west, straight through and out of town, up onto a snow-strewn plateau lit only by the moon. My headlights find the shiny globes of a doe's eyes just off the road. The radio has gone to static, and I've turned it to low, unable to bring myself to turn it off completely. A broken-down tractor marks the county road onto which I'm supposed to turn.

Ephraim's compound looks to be a trailer with add-on upon add-on cropping out from the original double-wide. A lone industrial light sends a shivery glow out from the house across the ice-and-gravel-encrusted driveway. It's not fear that greets me in the cold silence outside the car, but an undertone of disbelief—I have chosen to spend my Christmas Eve right here.

The taxidermist's picture taped up in the office all these months has led me to expect a much more imposing character than the man who opens the door. Ephraim is my height, at best, and rather slight in build. He stands before me in a tank top and jeans, his long, bleached hair held in a red bandanna.

"Merry Christmas," I say.

"Yeah. I'm just finishing up some work. Have yourself a beer or something."

"I'm Roxanne," I say.

"I know," he says, impatiently waving me in. "I'm not retarded."

He disappears down a narrow, dark hall leaving me alone in the faux-wood-paneled, galley-sized living room of the trailer, dimly lit and lined with stuffed creatures of all kinds. Eyes are everywhere—elk, deer, rabbits, raccoons—like a gothic hunting lodge. Their heads are macabre, but they have an impressive, lifelike subtlety in their poses. A large TV is perched on milk crates in the corner and a stereo is stacked with CDs—Led Zeppelin, Lynyrd Skynyrd, Boston, and REO Speedwagon. The banality of this setup makes me feel sorrier for him than I would if he were holed up in a rustic cabin without plumbing.

"I'll be out in five," he yells from down the hall.

"Take your time," I say too softly, and I'm about to repeat myself louder when he calls again.

"It's a Christmas gift. The guy's picking it up tomorrow morning. A buck head for his wife. It's pretty awesome. They live over in Helper. He's coming by at dawn."

I hear the clang of a dropped tool and the whirring of something electrical. It's tempting to venture back to see him in action, but I like to imagine the mad scientist at work. The couch is draped in a forest green bedsheet, which is tucked into the cushions, ash-spotted, and unevenly covering the yellow velour underneath. The room is like an old dorm room grown threadbare through twenty years of habitation. There is a tidiness in the way the magazines—*Car & Driver*, *Rolling Stone*—are piled neatly at the foot of the couch and every preserved animal has its own defined space. The vague, disagreeable pungence of formaldehyde lingers, mixed with old cigarettes and pine cleaner.

"I'll show you later," Ephraim says, as he comes back in, wiping his hands on a greasy towel. "The antlers are good. Real symmetrical."

"Great," I say.

"You look good," he says. "Are you new?"

"Pretty new," I say, deciding against reminding him I spoke with him on Thanksgiving. "Why do you ask?"

"I didn't recognize your description."

I'm expecting him to call me on its obvious stretches of the truth but he only seems pleased with himself that he was in the know.

"Have you always lived out here? In Nephi, I mean."

Ephraim goes into the kitchen.

"Yeah. I grew up with my grandparents over in Jerusalem, east of here on the edge of the Uinta, but since there's only fifty folks there, I've always said I'm from Nephi."

He returns with a beer can in each hand and holds one out to me.

"I was going to move down to Richfield some years ago to a bigger shop but that would have been a mistake. I got over it." Ephraim falls heavily into the couch beside me. "I need to be my own boss is the bottom line," he says, looking around at his animal companions.

"It's amazing work," I say. "So real-looking."

"Yep," he says. "I know. I'm not trying to brag or anything but I'm pretty much a master of the art."

"I can see you're right," I say, cracking open my Bud

Light. "Shall we get the money out of the way?"

"Hah," he says, shaking his head in exaggerated annoyance. "I should have known." Ephraim sits up with one hand on his knee, tilts his head back, and downs his beer, finishing with a shake of his hair. "What's the damage?" he asks, pulling a roll of bills from his jeans.

"Two hours. And then the travel fee. That comes to five hundred and forty."

"You've got to be shitting me!" he says, as if he didn't know, as if I might give him a special deal.

"You agreed to it over the phone."

"Sheesh," he says, shaking his head and counting out bills on his thigh. "Good thing it's Christmas Eve and I'm feeling generous." He hands me the money. "You can take off your coat. Throw it over the chair there. Want another beer?"

"No, not yet. Thanks."

After calling in to Marisa—she doesn't answer, so I act out the call in case he's listening—I start asking Ephraim questions, sensing his overwhelming desire to be heard. He's been percolating. With another beer, his words begin to flow, building to a sizable torrent.

"I didn't ever know my parents. My mom died when I was three, then my father bolted. Who knows what happened to him. I hope the fucker's dead. More likely down in Colorado City with ten wives. My grandfather kicked it when I was in high school and my grandma a few years back."

"You must miss having people around, out here on your own," I say resting my hand on his arm.

"Sometimes, I guess. I don't really notice it when I'm working but at night it's hard. I think most people think I don't have much to say. But I do. You know?"

"Yeah," I say.

He runs his fingers through his hair in rapid strokes and clears his throat to drown out the emotion.

"It's not that there aren't women," he says.

I don't ask him if there are any he doesn't pay for.

"I think they can't deal with my dedication to my work. They need too much attention." He loops his arm around my shoulders as if we are teenagers at the movies. "Taxidermy is my calling. My grandfather did it and I knew it was for me by age six. I've developed my own unique techniques. I have one guy who sends me his salmon all the way from Alaska because he thinks no one else makes the heads look so alive."

Ephraim's glistening face leads me to believe he is working up to a bigger move in my direction.

"Roxanne is a nice name," he says.

"Thank you."

"Do you want me to show you around the place?"

"Thought you'd never ask."

Ephraim points back to where the bedroom is but leads me instead into his workshop, awash in the greenish tinge of fluorescent light and the ghostly hush of lifelessness. There is a chemical tang to the air. White plastic

animal heads, grouped by species, line the walls. He pulls
out one of the drawers of what looks like a metal card catalog and glass eyeballs knock together as benignly as mar-
bles.

"These are imported from Germany," he says, holding
one up in his fingers. "They're for cats. Not the big wild
ones but house cats. For old ladies mostly."

I imagine the other escorts who have been here—
Jezebel bored and giggling, and Nikyla trying to be nice
despite finding it disturbing—as Ephraim points out the
different pelts drying on the line.

"Check this out," he says, motioning to a back table.

An enormous deer head looks up to the ceiling, its
giant, spiked branches of antlers wrapped in plastic.

"Wow," I say.

"I know, right? I bet this white tail was closing in on
seven years old."

"Do you ever do work for museums?" I ask.

Ephraim is so pleased with my question he can't hide
his smile as he bounces on his heels.

"I did an exhibit a couple years ago for the Salt Lake
zoo. Refurbishing this monkey diorama they have there.
That was cool. I like to go up there sometimes to visit it. I
did some good tail work on those guys."

I sit on a metal stool as he continues around the
studio: noses for any animal in plastic and rubber, the
drainage sink, scalpels, a whole drawer full of needles in
various sizes, nylon thread, cotton batting for stuffing that

he orders from furniture upholstering wholesalers because he says it looks more realistic under the skin than what his suppliers in the trade offer. He pets a half-stuffed raccoon whose body is frozen in an inquisitive pose, as if it's just about to peer into a window.

"Can I watch you work?" I ask.

And from his sad smile I know that my request is the nicest thing he has heard in a long while, edging into intimate territory that has always been his solitary and passionate pursuit.

"Uh, yeah. Sure," he says. "It's pretty neat stuff. This guy here," he says, massaging the back fur of the raccoon, "used to scavenge in Mr. Moses's garbage cans, so he finally took him out with a baby .22. See this bare spot in the fur right here? I filled it in with some rubber molding and now I'm going to graft fur onto it. There. See? You'd never know, would you?"

I smile and shake my head "no."

"I already picked out his eyes, so I paint some adhesive around the rims, push them through some, adjust, and voilà."

The wind finds the small space between the window and its frame, blowing through in cold wisps that seek out my exposed neck. I let my hair down to combat the chill.

"The head is probably the best part. You squeeze the skull form into the face skin from below—when it's a good fit, it pops right into place—move it around so the eyes and nose sit right, and then you're ready to sew. Don't get the wrong idea, though. I've worked on this one for hours already. Even the ears and whiskers required some refurbishing."

The gusts outside make a cooing sound as they whoosh by the house.

"Are you cold?" he asks.

I nod.

Ephraim reaches into a trunk and pulls out a large dark furry hide.

"A black bear. Back when it was still legal to kill them. That'll warm you right up."

A beastly essence still clings to the skin and I have to breathe through my mouth when he drapes it around my shoulders.

"Don't worry, he's been dead for about ten years."

I'm not sure what he thinks I might be worried about but I let it go. He places the raccoon upside down in a padded chamois-covered vice and threads a large curved needle like the kind used for quilting. His hands work in graceful tandem with delicate precision, his stitches as even as those of a seasoned seamstress.

"This is one of the secrets," he says. "Most people rush through this part. But the whole point is to leave no mark."

"You have nice hands," I say.

Ephraim stops sewing and looks up at me, suddenly self-conscious and momentarily out of his element.

"Yeah?" he asks, his face pink.

"Sorry. I didn't mean to interrupt."

He stitches quickly now, up the throat, and with some intricate maneuver with the needle at the underside of the neck, Ephraim closes it up and snips the thread.

"Feel it," he says. "Run your finger along here."

Ephraim guides my finger with his hand along the almost invisible seam.

"Massage the fur so it moves over the stitches like this."

He demonstrates, I follow, and then his hand covers mine. The fur is rougher than I expected.

"What now?" I ask.

"I'll spray it tomorrow with this superfine-mist oil treatment, mount him, and he'll be ready to go."

"No, I mean, what now?" I try to be seductive but my voice sounds too tinny.

"Oh," he says, pulling away, rubbing his palms together. "Okay then."

He points his head toward the hall and lifts his eyebrows in question. I hop off the stool and follow him into the house.

His bedroom is small and spare except for the giant floor-to-ceiling photographic mountain scene covering one wall.

"Pretty badass, huh? I put that up last year. It comes in large sheets like wallpaper. I've seen this one that's a view of the Grand Canyon. I might change it up."

Both of us stand stiffly in the middle of the room.

"Maybe we could light some candles in here," I say, spying one next to the bed.

He jumps into action, pulling an array of fruity drug-store candles from his dresser drawer.

"Much better," he says as he lights them. I turn off the overhead light.

I'm glad there are no animals in here to watch us.

"Why don't we sit on the bed," I say.

I think Ephraim is relieved to be told what to do. He sits gingerly on the edge of the bed and I run my hand down his back. He closes his eyes and surrenders a deep, pent-up breath.

"There," I say.

My hand travels onto his neck, slowly rubbing, venturing up into his hair and down across his collarbone. I kick off my shoes and move behind him to work with two hands, slowly kneading, one inch at a time. His breath catches and I realize that he's crying.

"Baby, what's wrong?" I say softly near his ear, hugging him from behind.

Ephraim forces a stop to the tears with a few emphatic breaths.

"Roxanne. This is just so…nice."

I brush his hair behind his ear.

"Ephraim, would you like to kiss me?"

He turns to me and nods, looking like a plaintive boy with a skinned knee.

*

Ephraim is earnest and aggressive and incredibly

appreciative all at the same time. He yanks off my clothes then stops for a look of grateful rapture at the sight of my skin. Still in his jeans, he humps my leg and squeezes my breasts as if they're made of Silly Putty.

"Slow," I say. "We're in no hurry."

He stops, rises up to look at me, but then he's at it again, tugging at my bra without knowing how to get it unhooked. I do it for him because it's Christmas Eve, because he's a fine taxidermist, and because, I realize, I don't care that much one way or the other.

"Roxanne, would you mind if I took my pants off?" he asks in a polite, quiet voice.

"I wouldn't mind, Ephraim. I'll help," I say.

And in trembling candlelight, with the flash of his needy eyes as he kisses my stomach, I calculate that his desire to have me is, at that moment, greater than my desire not to be had. I'm weary. I tell myself that it will mean more to him to have sex with me than it will for me not to.

And so I guide him to me.

After a few minutes of flailing about, Ephraim looks down in exasperation at his only semi-erect penis. Even in the stingy light of the room, I see shame in his eyes. He flips me around beneath him so that I am face-down on the bed, and I'm flooded with the sour bodily smell of dirty sheets. I squelch a gag and he thrusts himself against me with singular intent. When he shifts on top of me, I can manage only shallow breaths, each tinged with the smell of his ripe sweat. I resign myself to the disaster that barrels toward me.

He is rough. It hurts. But I don't resist. I feel like it's easier just to get it over with, get to the other side. I tune out his grunts and his slick, heaving body. I close my eyes and remove myself. I teeter on the verge of emotional vertigo but concentrate on the promise of release. I wait for the aftermath of calm.

I focus on a Christmas twenty-three years ago when my sister and I got a new sled. It was orange plastic with a yellow rope and grooved runners for speed. Behind our house, the gently sloping yard was our designated hill. It was a nice easy ride, fun the first few times, but soon dull. The boys next door were racing down their cleared ravine and shooting across the iced-over pond at its base. We were prohibited from joining them, which was fine for my sister, but the boys' exhilarating whoops proved too tempting for me. I don't remember much of my ride but I can't forget holding on for life, with the icy air making my eyes water, and then sliding to shore and looking up, and seeing my father appear at the top of the hill.

With an angry grip on my upper arm, he led me back to the house, where I received a stinging succession of spankings, and then I cried and cried—not for the pain, but for the injustice. He punished me for the danger. For an accident that never happened. I remember his woodsy smell of Scotch and the patchy antiseptic overlay of Listerine.

*

When I open my eyes, I'm met with the sight of Ephraim's unruly hair and postcoital blush. He shyly covers his lower half with the sheet, minding our separation on the bed.

"So. I suppose I got to pay some extra for that," he says.

"There isn't exactly a pay scale," I say, sitting up.

"Can I get you anything?" he asks.

"No thanks," I say. I don't want to be here another minute.

He bites the tip of his finger, camouflaging a smile, which I take to mean he enjoyed it enough for the both of us.

"I don't suppose you'd like to do this again sometimes. I mean, not for money."

"Thanks...but I don't think so."

"I guess Nephi is kind of far from Salt Lake."

From the small digital clock by the bed, I can see that our two hours have almost elapsed. I search around the sheets for my underwear.

"Well. I best be on my way," I say pulling them on.

He turns his crestfallen face away, sits up, and grabs his jeans from the floor.

"Put your hand out," he says.

I lose count of the bills.

"Don't spend it all in one place," he says, his shell of bravado again intact.

His semen pools in my underwear.

"Say, how come you do this, anyway? You seem like a nice girl," he says.

I put on my skirt and wrinkled blouse.

"Does one preclude the other?" I ask.

"What?"

"Nothing. I'm just doing it for now."

"Well, drive safe."

"Okay. Merry Christmas."

"Yeah, it is, isn't it?" He sighs. "Oh wait a second. I have something for you."

He jogs down the hall toward his workshop. I hear the sounds of a door and drawers and indecision. I'd almost forgotten about the fox pelt. But when he returns, he's holding a majestic silver fox mounted on a block of shined walnut.

"I want you to have this," he says.

And with that, I take the gift, hugging it to my chest, and greet the freezing darkness of Christmas morning. I heave the fox out the window somewhere near Spring Lake.

*

I nod off twice on the drive back from Nephi, the second time narrowly missing the guardrail and an indeterminate drop-off outside of American Fork. I cross into Salt Lake City and I'm too exhausted to go home and think about my choices and the money in my pocket, so I go straight to the office instead. The sound of my slammed car door punctuates the still, predawn alley and my heels clack against the frozen sidewalk. I let myself in and lock the door behind me.

Someone has left the Christmas tree lights on, blinking with false gaiety. The cold air is stale with smoke and perfume, and I pull the heat lever all the way to the right. I unplug the lights, leaving total darkness, and I sit there motionless. My underwear is crusty and I am sore. The only sound is the tired heater churning out the dry hot air.

chapter 18

The phone wakes me at ten a.m. My face is stuck to the leather cushion and my legs are hanging over the armrest. Sweat has gathered between my breasts and my mouth is cottony, my lips cracked. It's so hot I'm disoriented and I throw my coat off and stagger to the heater. Ninety-five degrees. I drink rust-tinged water straight from the bathroom tap. I hear the phone ringing again as I begin to regain my equilibrium.

I half expect McCallister or Ford, or Ephraim even, but it's a man calling from Miami, his voice rushed and sheepish, stained with something I pinpoint as guilt, wanting to pay for an escort to keep his great-uncle company for an hour or two on Christmas. Emigration Canyon. Will pay in advance with a credit card, including a hundred-dollar tip.

"But you can't tell him you're being paid," he says.

I feel dirty and confused. Last night I had sex for money for no good reason.

"I'm sorry," I say. "I don't understand."

"Make something up. I don't know. Say you're Doreen's daughter's friend."

"But—"

"Say it's some type of outreach. Church group. He won't ask."

Although I'm curious about the reason behind this man's request, in the end, it doesn't really matter. I agree to the date. I have a job to do, and a growing list of things I don't want to think about.

Unable to stay disassociated from my life any longer, I reluctantly go home, shed my well-worn clothes onto the floor, and use all the hot water in a long, scalding shower. My skin smarts and reddens, and I scrub until it's tender. I'm glad I can't see myself in the steamed mirror. After I dry, I pull on jeans, a sweatshirt, and sneakers and tie my hair tightly in a ponytail. No lace underwear. No makeup. No perfume. I down three glasses of water and slide the mound of twenties from Ephraim under my pillow.

I could really use breakfast—the meal of hope and things still to be done—but Ruth's is dark when I pass by and I drive on toward my assignment, my stomach bitter and empty.

The house is simple, rough-hewn and neat, like a prairie pioneer home might have looked. Instead of a doorbell there is a cowbell hanging from the porch eave, which I ring, awakening the whole quiet canyon. Silence returns. After a couple minutes, there is a shuffling sound and the door opens.

The right side of the man's face sags and his right hand curls like a hook. In his left hand he holds a pad of paper and pencil. He writes, "May I help you?" holding the pad up to face me.

"Hi," I say. "Merry Christmas. I'm Jane." I don't notice the slip until I see him write my real name.

"Hello, Jane," he writes. "I'm Virgil Samuelson."

I shake his proffered healthy hand and smile.

"So. Um. I'm a friend of Doreen's daughter from church? I thought I'd drop by and say hello. I don't have any family in the area either."

Virgil squints and tilts his head, doubting my story yet pleased enough to have the company. He motions me inside with his good hand.

A pronounced limp makes his movements slow and jerky, but there is something elegant in his manner too. He is kind and a shadow of subtle stateliness surrounds him. The home is spare with Shaker furniture and arts-and-crafts-style details in the woodwork and molding. There is a fire going in the living room and Beethoven on the record player. Virgil points to his teacup and then to me.

"Yes. Thank you. That would be nice," I say.

After he returns with my tea, we sit in matching wing-back chairs angled in toward the fire.

"Are you from here?" I ask.

He shakes his head "no." I try to envision how his face must have looked before it fell.

He writes, "Chicago. Came here after stroke."

"Why here?"

My tone causes him to grunt a laugh.

"Brother was here," he scrawls.

"I'm originally from a suburb of Cleveland. Before here, New York," I say.

He rolls his hand at me to elicit more.

I talk and he listens, smiling now and then with one side of his mouth. I tell him this is the first Christmas I haven't gone home, how Utah has been an adjustment, that I like his house. It is soothing to talk and he seems content to listen. I tell him about my parents, my sister, my childhood, my college years. Every time I pause to let him interject, he motions me onward, long ago having put down his pad. At a certain point I'm not even sure he's listening as he stares at the flames, finishing his tea. By the time I get to why I moved to Utah, Virgil is fast asleep in his chair. I sit for a time as the fire dies down. My tea is cold. I watch him as he sleeps, his head lolling to the side, drool glistening on his downcast lip. I'm exhausted and hungry. It occurs to me that I could be close to being untethered. I'm living a life I barely recognize as my own.

I make my way quietly to the kitchen, hoping to find something to appease my gnawing stomach. I prepare a small plateful of pepper crackers and aged cheddar, add a couple of gingerbread men on the side, and eat standing at the sink surveying the backyard. There is a curious small building on the property, a cross between a shed and a cottage. After a quick check on my still-sleeping host I slip out the back.

The door to the structure is unlocked. When I finally find the light switch, a deep ruby bulb turns on revealing what appears to be a darkroom. Pinned to a drying line is photograph upon photograph in black-and-white of an old enameled colander, with varying degrees of contrast and shadow, at slightly different angles, with light shooting though its holes like water from a showerhead. They are striking images, stark and dramatic. On the counter are boxes containing more pictures: an old work boot, a knife, an egg, a lamp, a dead bird, a rock, a plate, a window. Still life after still life. No people. Mesmerizing and lonely. I can't stop staring. I consume them. I pull out boxes from all over the room for more. A tire, a doorknob, a tree stump, an artichoke, and then at the bottom of the last box, three photographs of the curled hand, clawlike and withered, with the slightest hint of blurred movement in the fingers.

I wonder if these are his secret, if he has anyone in his life, what he did before the stroke, if there is any way that he is happy. I leave the mess I've made as it is.

Inside, Virgil is still asleep.

"Dear Virgil," I write on his pad. "You take beautiful photographs. Merry Christmas. Jane."

chapter 19

For days all I do is sleep. When I wake up, I take Tylenol PMs until I sleep again. I tell Mohammed I have a fever of 103. I wait for Ember to come back but she doesn't. Even though I try not to, my thoughts return to my night with Ephraim again and again. I don't know what to make of it. I don't know what to make of me. I am eroding. When I finally crawl back into Premier to work the phones on New Year's Eve, I say I've had some kind of terrible virus.

Ford calls and tells me that Ember left him and Moab the day after Christmas. She said she felt too confined, too tied down. She said she needed to find her life on her own before she could latch onto someone else. Ford recognized her ill-tempered manner and fierce headaches as the beginnings of withdrawal, so when he woke up to find Ember foraging around in the dark for her car keys, it was not altogether unexpected. On the phone he sounds composed, almost fatalistic, but beneath it is a hollowness that comes from being left. I picture him as he calls from the gas station payphone, looking around at the purple sky and the dusty asphalt, feeling like he doesn't understand the world at all.

I'm pretty sure Ember is here in Salt Lake, it being the closest city she knows where to score. She's been a no-show at Premier and Mohammed just shakes his head at yet another one to let him down.

I check the parks first, Liberty and Pioneer, then drive by the coffee place at Ninth and Ninth, the eerie downtown mall, Temple Square—all the places I know she likes, looking for her beat-up Saab and those heat-emitting eyes. I fear that she is in trouble, but I also fear that she has discharged me along with Ford and it was that easy for her to let me go too. I catch what looks to be a familiar walk and the right kind of hair but as I drive nearer, the girl turns out to be a teenager with a baby strapped to her front.

It's only four o'clock but I follow a hunch to the Zephyr, figuring the bar is as good a place to find her as any and maybe I'll have a beer to settle myself in the process. When my eyes adjust to the low lights, I see Ember perched on a stool at the end of the bar, her slight frame even slighter, her hands making frenetic gestures as she relays something to the bartender. At first I'm angry, then I check myself and remember how glad I am that she is not hurt or worse.

"Hey," I say, trying to sound casual.

She turns and a trace of panic sparks her shadowed eyes.

"Jane," she says. "I'm so glad to see you."

My look betrays my skepticism.

"No, I am. I mean, yeah, I was avoiding you a tiny bit. I didn't want you to be disappointed or mad or whatever." There's dirt under her chewed fingernails. Her face twitches and highlights a vacancy I haven't seen before. She slides from the stool and encircles my neck with her spindly arms.

"I was worried," I say into her smoky hair.

"That's not allowed," she says. "And not necessary. Lord knows, I'm a big girl."

There is a new distance between us.

"I bet Mohammed's pretty pissed," she says, getting me to laugh.

"I talked to Ford," I say.

"It was best, you know. For me to end it with him."

But what about me, I want to ask.

"Where are you staying?" I ask her instead.

She shrugs. "Here and there. The past couple nights with my friend Steve downtown, just west of the tracks."

It's the first I've heard of Steve.

"You'd like him. He's funny. And he's not afraid of just going. Taking off on an adventure."

"You can stay with me, you know, whenever you want," I say. I know I sound desperate, like one of the johns wanting to appear blasé when really he would do anything to have her stay with him longer, not because she's getting paid but because she wants to.

"I know," Ember says.

She has already cut me loose.

"I have this really great thing to tell you about," she says with a sudden mood shift, rubbing her nose. "Steve has this gig coming up—he's a drummer—in Spain and I think I'm going to go with him. Cool, right? Barcelona in the spring, dancing, tapas, bullfights. I've always wanted to go to Spain."

She so genuinely craves the renewal her fantasy offers that I want to swaddle her in a blanket and carry her home.

"Hey," she says sharply. "Don't look at me like that. You of anyone know why I need to go. Don't give me that shit." I can't tell if it's bitterness or being strung out that gives her words their bite. "It's not what you think. Sometimes it's just better to change the scenery. Fresh start and all that."

I squeeze her in another hug. I want to get to her but I can't.

"Okay," I say.

"Yeah. Okay," she says.

"You know where to find me," I say. "When you want."

"And you'll know where to find me," she says, having regained her footing.

"I will?"

"Running with the bulls." Ember downs the rest of her beer and slams it on the bar.

"Sweet Home Alabama" starts playing on the jukebox.

"Come on," she says, grabbing my hand. "Let's dance."

I know that Ember is doing what she does but it makes me feel worse, like I could be anybody.

"I have to go," I say.

She holds my eyes but I look away first.

"Okay," she says.

She kisses my cheek and lets go of my hand.

*

Ember drives over to my apartment later that night to clear out the rest of her things. Not much is there, really, just some clothes, a sketch pad and some makeup. She looks so hungry standing there in my kitchen I make her scrambled eggs.

We take our coffee out to the front stoop

"I'll send you a postcard from the Costa Brava," she says.

"I'd like that," I say.

"I sure won't miss winter," Ember says. She can't sit still, first shaking her foot then scratching at a rough patch on her elbow. "I'm going to go get my stuff and put it in the car. Be right back."

Of course she's inside for longer than she needs to be, but I let it go. After she returns, she throws her bag into the front seat and leans against the car for a moment looking at me.

"Hey, Jane," she says, "watch this."

With legs straight and toes pointed, Ember cartwheels across the snowy lawn with true grace. I soak up that joyful image, to fend off the sadness that is sure to come. When she reaches me, she rocks dizzily on her feet, but then smiles.

"Bravo," I say.

"And with that, Queen Jane, I leave you," she announces, curtsying like a ballerina.

It's hard to even fake a smile. I stand and pull her to me, kissing each cheek and then her forehead with loud smacks. Then, as only Ember can do, she kisses me softly on the lips, I melt, and she's gone.

*

I sleep fitfully and wake to a morning curiously warm and humid for the desert winter. By the time I reach the car, I'm sweating in my ill-chosen down jacket. The lake smell is heavy and sulfurous even way out here in the Avenues, and in my pre-coffee haze, it makes me woozy. When I get to the Coffee Garden, it dawns on me that it's Saturday and I have the day off. But I go to work anyway if only to keep my ruminations at bay and to not be alone. As I arrive at the office, balancing cup and steering wheel in one hand, I spill coffee on my lap. I dump the rest out onto the sidewalk, melting a brown hole into a mound of already dirty slush.

Diamond, Nikyla, and Jezebel are sprawled morosely on the couches watching Bugs Bunny.

"Hey," I say.

"Hey," the three say in unison.

Nikyla pulls a few strands of her hair through her fingers looking at the split ends in the light and Jezebel bites her thumbnail. Diamond scrunches down lower in the couch.

"Who died?" I ask.

"Diamond slept at my house because her husband is a dick," Nikyla says pointing next to her. "And Jezebel's car broke down this morning and it's going to cost eight hundred dollars to fix. And she has her period."

"Being a girl totally sucks," Jezebel says.

"And I feel like I'm going to puke," Nikyla says.

"I'll work for one of you if you want," I say.

Jezebel raises her eyebrow at me. "That's weird. If I didn't so need the money," she says.

Diamond stands and stretches with a loud yawn. "I'm not that generous. I'm outta here. We'll see if the asshole's in a better mood. Later girls."

I squeeze myself in the warm space Diamond left between Jezebel and Nikyla.

"Do you mean it, Rox?" Nikyla asks.

"Yeah," I say. "Go home. Feel better."

"That's so cool. I owe you," she says.

"No you don't," I say. "You'd do the same for me."

"Jezebel," Marisa says from the desk, "Jason Butler wants to see you at the Dream Inn."

"Cheap bastard," she says.

*

There was a time around the age of ten that I became obsessed with the vulnerability of my parents. My aunt had just died of cancer, and a neighbor had just been killed in a car accident. I didn't worry about what could happen to me, but I would lie awake fearing all the bad things that could happen to my mom and dad and how dependent on them I was. I obsessed about the practical day-to-day things—Who would pick me up from school? Who would take my temperature? How would I cook dinner? I knew my teenaged sister would just move in with her friends and leave me to fend for myself.

I asked God to please just let my parents live until I was twenty, because then I'd be an adult and I'd be able to manage. And when I made this deal, I was relieved. But then one afternoon, I mentioned to my mom that I would be an adult in exactly ten years.

"If only it were that easy," she said. "I wish there were some magic number. Unfortunately some people, no matter how old they get, never become adults."

Her disillusioning words wedged into my memory like a splinter, gestating unease. The thought has stuck with me that maybe I never quite made it, never crossed the threshold. I missed what everyone else around me seemed to get. I was a bluffer. Destined to be on the outside, going through the motions, pretending.

*

I am awakened by Marisa—I fell asleep during a show about sharks—to go see "Ricky Martin" at the Motel 6 on North Temple out toward the airport. After a quick gargle with the community mouthwash, I'm off.

When the guy opens the door, all he has on is a bed-sheet wrapped low around his waist. He's tall and lean, with ropy, muscled arms, olive skin, and a menacing-looking pointed goatee. He stands there with an idiotic grin.

"Ricky?" I ask, and he laughs and pulls me into the room.

"Aren't you something," he says. "Let's see your little tits." He grabs my chest through my sweater.

"Whoa there," I say, pulling away. "Why don't we get the money out of the way first."

While he fishes in his wallet, I catch a glimpse of his license. The name, Sam Gomez, I recognize from our 86ed list. But I'm not alarmed. I'm pretty sure he's on it for bad checks.

"Cash only," I say.

"Yeah, yeah," he says, counting out twenties. "There's extra in there for you."

"Thanks," I say, shoving two hundred dollars into my pocket.

As I call in to Marisa, I watch as he reclines on the bed and greedily sucks down a cigarette.

"Are you safe?" she asks.

"Yeah," I say.

"Have you collected?"

"Yep," I say, patting my pocket.

"Get your cute ass over here," he says as he snuffs out his cigarette.

I put my game face on, take off my coat, and pull my sweater over my head. My breasts in my hands, I move my hips in small circles.

"Yeah. I could tell you liked to party. Get those off now," he says, pointing to my jeans.

I strip down to my bra and underwear and straddle him on the bed. He is naked. I touch my cold feet to his thighs to warm them. We start to kiss and he smells like beer and aftershave. His tongue is rough, groping as far into my mouth as he can. With one hand on my neck he forces me down on my back with the whole of his body. There is sweat on his forehead and his penis is hard against my hip.

His forcefulness is sudden and startling. I try to diffuse it.

"Baby," I say. "I want to watch you."

He ignores me and crushes my breasts together, grinding himself against my stomach.

"Come on now," I say.

He reaches for his pants and I hear the telltale sound of a condom wrapper. I try to move away but he has me pinned. Some of the guys like to ejaculate in a condom to keep the whole thing cleaner but I'm starting to sense he has something else in mind.

"You don't want to break the rules," I coo to him. I try

to swallow my rising panic.

"Fuck the rules. What do you think I paid you for?" he says with a nasty smile. "That's a lot of money to jack off. I could have stayed home and done it for free."

His body covers mine and he's squeezing my wrists, cutting off the blood to my hands. I can barely breathe. I consider giving in—it's not like I haven't done this before—to get it over with as quickly as possible.

I stop writhing and lay still as he rips down my underwear and wedges his knees between my legs.

"That's right," he says. "You be a good sport now."

All at once the weight of his words strikes me as viscerally as if I were punched. I gasp for insufficient breath, infused with the dry burn of rage. The realization of the wrongness of the moment, the surfacing understanding that this is not what I want, breaks into focus with the clarity of pure will. I am remembering something I didn't think I knew. This is not me. I am not this. My still, small voice says, "Save yourself, goddamn it."

I start to fight and scream.

"Get off me!" I yell over and over.

I owe him nothing. I flail at him with any part of me I can get free. I butt him with my head. He lets go of one of my wrists and cracks the back of his hand across my cheek, but it only incites me further. I dig my heels into the mattress for leverage and with my free hand, grasp for anything. I can feel the venom of his fury, and I think if I stop moving, rape would be just the beginning.

Somehow I get the clock radio in my hand, and with newfound strength, bash a corner of it into his temple. And again and again with everything I have.

"Fuck," he yells, shielding his head.

He is momentarily dazed enough for me to wriggle out from under him.

"Fucking whore," he says, "my head. Jesus."

He swings wildly at me but misses, collapsing back onto the bed as blood seeps into his eye. I scoop my heap of clothes in my arms and run out into the frozen afternoon, so high on survival I don't even feel my nakedness or the icy asphalt on the soles of my feet.

chapter 20

Detective Logan, who interviewed me to get licensed, is writing in one of those old-fashioned reporter's notebooks, leaning against the wall in the office. I sit in the middle of the love seat.

Mohammed lurks nearby with his arms crossed looking sullen and befuddled. Marisa is red-eyed from crying, she will be issued a misdemeanor for admitting she didn't go through the correct screening procedures. I'm flushed and tired in the hot office, relieved, yet at the same time, secretly exhilarated. I have emerged with something new. I feel I could lift a car or run a marathon or faint at any minute. My hands shake.

"This shouldn't be a surprise to any of you," Logan says, as if addressing an audience. "It's the nature of this business. You're playing roulette. And I'll tell you, even though we arrested this guy, I'm pretty sure nothing will ever come of it. No matter what kind of evidence we have against him, the bottom line is you're an escort," he says, pointing at me.

My cheek throbs hot where I was hit. Bruises have settled in around my wrists, angry and red with deepening patches of purple. The doctor said superficial injuries. No evidence of sexual trauma.

"I think I'm done for now," Logan says, flipping closed his notebook. "You should have stuck to the phone," he says to me.

I don't say anything in response. He shakes his head in disgust before pulling the door shut behind him.

"Roxanne," Mohammed says. "Come with me please."

I follow him back into his sad little office.

"I am sorry that this happened to you," he says. "But I'm glad that you are fine. You are an adult. I think it's best not to blow it out of proportion in front of the other girls. They look up to you, you know. They will be looking to you."

He fills out a check to me for five hundred dollars.

"Take this for your trouble," he says.

I forgive Mohammed his facile recompense because I have to believe he doesn't know any better. But I need something different.

"Can you tell me where Nikyla lives? She's not answering her phone," I say.

"Listen, everyone knows the risks," he says. "It will pass. It will go away. Do not cause a greater disturbance."

"I need her address. You have it. It's a small request. Considering."

"I cannot give it to you," he says, rubbing his forehead. "You know that it is not allowed. Just go home. Get some sleep. You will feel better." Mohammed looks tired in his atypically rumpled suit.

I go to the dented drawer that I know holds his shoddy personnel files and he makes no effort to stop me. Each wrinkled application has a Polaroid stapled to it that I have to use as a guide, since I don't know Nikyla's real name. Face after face, girl after girl, the endless stream. Hopeful eyes, sorrowful smiles, rouged cheeks, freckled noses, scornful lips, blank faces. I recognize very few. Toward the back I find a picture of a younger-looking Nikyla, proud and sure, unsmiling, stapled to Diana Nelson's application.

Mohammed stares out through the dusty blinds of his small window.

*

I find the nondescript stucco apartment complex behind Red Lobster and across the street from the Fred Meyer Superstore. It's rundown, and plastic children's toys litter the snow-spotted grounds and cracked sidewalk. I ring 2A.

"What," a young male voice barks through the staticky intercom.

"Um, yeah, hi. Is Diana home? It's Roxanne."

There is the sound of a background exchange and the door buzzes open. I go up the stairs and down a scuffed beige-walled hall. Nikyla's boyfriend, in a baseball hat, opens the door and with a teenager's tiny head-flick greeting, points into the living room where Nikyla is slouched in sweatpants on the couch watching TV.

"I'm going out, baby," he says to her, grabbing his parka from the coat tree.

"Bring treats," she calls as the door shuts.

"Hey," I say quietly.

"Hey Rox. This is a surprise. What's up?"

"I had a crazy day," I say.

"Is something wrong?"

"I had some trouble this morning on a date. I was kind of attacked."

Nikyla holds her hand to her mouth.

"But I got away," I say. "I'm fine. I fought him off."

"Oh my God," she says, getting up to hug me. "Come here and sit down."

The room has little more than the TV and a couch, peach wall-to-wall carpeting and a Monet poster tacked above a stereo on the floor. The shades are all drawn and thin light filters through the gaps.

I exhale heavily, feeling worn and used up. Nikyla enfolds me in a knit throw.

"I am so sorry," she says. "Shit, shit, shit. It was my shift. It should have been me."

"Don't say that, okay? It shouldn't have been anyone."

She pulls me to her and rocks me against her chest.

"Are you okay?"

"I'm okay," I say. "It was Sam Gomez from the 86ed list."

"Fucking motherfucker."

"In a second he had me."

"Oh, look at your wrists. That bastard. How'd you get away?"

"Whacked him in the head with a clock radio."

"Awesome," she says.

"Nikyla—Diana—you shouldn't do this anymore. It's not worth it."

She says nothing for a beat, which I take to mean she gets it but I haven't changed her mind.

"I'm not supposed to say anything yet, but I'm four weeks along," she says, touching her stomach. "I just found out."

"A baby?" I say.

She squeezes my hand.

"I think it's going to be a girl. I'm hoping. I'm named after Princess Diana, so I thought it would be cool to call my daughter Spencer. Spencer Brewster. That's Josh's last name."

"I like it," I say. "It sounds like a movie-star name."

"What's your real name anyway?" Nikyla asks.

"Jane," I say, and for the first time all day, tears come.

"That fits you so much better," she says.

*

After hearing what happened, Jezebel arrives with a

stack of videos and a huge bag from Taco Bell. Albee yips and races around the room.

"First is *Save the Last Dance*," Jezebel says, "then *Pretty Woman*. Duh. Then we go get Twizzlers and come back for the best movie of all time."

"With the hottest guy ever," Nikyla says.

"*Reality Bites*," they say together.

"Oh, I got those pants for you," Nikyla says to Jezebel. "Remind me after the movie."

"Sweet," Jezebel says. "I'll pay you back after my next shift."

I lean my head against the back of the couch and Albee climbs into my lap. I feel like the brittle husk that has surrounded me has cracked open.

Jezebel pushes Play.

"I wish I had hit my uncle with a clock radio," she says as she squeezes in on my right, securing me between them.

chapter 21

Before Utah was a state, the LDS church proposed naming the new territory Deseret, a term from the Book of Mormon meaning "honeybee." This struck Brigham Young as an appropriate symbol of the Mormons' industry and their belief of working for the good of the collective whole. Although Congress named the state Utah, after the Ute Indians of the region, Mormons continued to call their homeland the Kingdom of Deseret. Today the beehive symbol is inscribed on everything from highway signs to the official state seal of Utah, and to my surprise, as I examine it closely for the first time, my escort license.

It's been three days since my run-in with Sam Gomez. I haven't been in to the office and I wonder how long it will be before I get a call. I put my license back in my wallet, turn out the light, and try to envision what this valley must have looked like to those Mormon pioneers looking down on it from the east. New and vast and strange.

Ten minutes later, just as I'm on the blurry edge of sleep, the doorbell rings.

It's McCallister.

I'm shocked—deep down I thought his threat was all talk and way too much of an effort. Something leaps in me at the sight of him but then it ebbs as I place the feeling as familiarity and nothing more. He looks shorter than I remember him, thinner. Less. In my memory he has a certain radiance that his presence lacks. It strikes me that he's from a part of my life that no longer exists.

"Surprise," he says, leaning against the doorway.

"I can't believe you," I say.

"You look good, Jane. Exile suits you," he says.

"Sure," I say, looking down at the snowman-patterned pajamas my mom sent me for Christmas.

"That temple is freaky looking. Like a sci-fi castle."

"So let me guess. She dumped you."

"She threw a snow globe at me that narrowly missed my forehead," he says. "Took a chunk out of the wall."

"You always did like her flair for the dramatic," I say.

"It's freezing out here. Aren't you going to ask me in?" he asks.

I look at him, oblivious. He is unaware of so much.

"Come on. What is this? Do you want me to beg?"

I stand aside and hold open the door.

"Aren't you going to ask me how I've been?" I ask.

"Okay. How are you? What have you been up to?"

"Oh, I've been pretty good. I started having sex for

money," I say. But now that I've said it I don't have the energy to really say it, to make him understand. I pull my pajama cuffs into my hands, over the yellowing bruises on my wrists.

"What?" he laughs. "As if." He drops his duffel bag, and takes off his coat, already having moved on from the thought.

"You don't know everything," I say. But I'm glad he doesn't bite. I hang his coat in the closet.

Standing in the middle of my living room, McCallister looks puzzled, young, despite his sun-creased eyes. The overhead light is bright and unflattering.

"Where's all your stuff?" he asks. "I always pictured you here with your old red couch and that weird painting you had in your kitchen."

"I left most of it on the sidewalk when I left. I got a lot of this from the Mormon thrift store."

McCallister looks decidedly out of place.

"I thought Ford's girlfriend was living with you," he says.

"She left. But when she was here she usually slept in the bed with me."

"Is there something you want to tell me?"

"What are you doing here anyway?" I ask.

"What do you think? I'm here to pick out some wives."

I cross my arms.

"Of course I'm here to see you," he says.

"I told you on the phone. There's nothing for you here."

He stares.

"You can't stay," I say.

"Oh come on, Jane."

And for the first time, I feel sorry for him. He looks bewildered in unfamiliar terrain.

From the hall closet I hand him a pillow and a blanket.

"Sofa city, sweetheart," I say. "We can talk in the morning."

My bedroom door has been closed for less than five minutes—my head swamped with conflicting wants—before McCallister knocks and pushes it open. I'm about to say "no way" but I want the closeness and obfuscation of body to body, with no threat, and no surprises.

And because I want to, I say, "Okay."

I pull back the covers and he scampers in, looping me in a spooning hug. In the dark, I know his body instantly. He kisses my neck over and over. It feels like an apology and I accept it.

I remember the smell of Ephraim's sheets and the strawberry candle and the sound of his frantic grunts. Sam Gomez's thick tongue in my mouth. No. I force my mind blank but my body tenses.

"Is this okay?" McCallister says.

"Yes," I say.

His hands know just where to go; they are confident and deft but not groping or overbearing. I relax with his touch and let myself feel good. I always loved how he took charge. I close my eyes and feel his palms against my breasts, my back, my stomach. Warm, solid, knowing. We don't speak. The sex has the sad and sweet quality of one long good-bye. And through it all, I know that he's no longer what I need.

*

We lie side by side looking at the shadows of tree branches on the ceiling. I know he senses that I have retreated.

"I'm not angry at you anymore," I say.

"I must be really good," he says.

"I'm serious."

"I know."

"But I haven't changed my mind," I say.

"I came here for you," he says.

"No, you came here for you," I say.

"We're good for each other, Jane."

"Even you know that's not true."

McCallister shakes his head.

"There's an oral tradition of the Utes," I say. "Ghosts happen when people haven't been buried properly."

"What are you talking about?"

"I think we're each other's ghost. We haven't buried each other, so we linger. But I think that maybe it's time."

He rolls away from me, and I don't do anything to bring him back.

"This is it for me," I say.

"You're the only person who makes me feel okay," he says.

"Tough shit," I say. "Maybe it's time for me to feel okay."

McCallister is speechless. He rubs his forehead and then his whole face.

"What happened to you?" he asks. "I thought you'd be happy. I thought it's what you wanted."

I don't answer.

He throws off the comforter and grabs his T-shirt and boxers from the floor. With his hand on the doorknob, he stops and turns back to me.

"Jane?"

"Yeah?"

"Maybe if you come back to New York we could try again?"

I am quiet and he pulls the door shut.

When I awake the next morning, McCallister is rustling around in the other room. With one word, I could change everything. If I said his name, he would come back. But I choose not even to say good-bye. I close my eyes. I hear him zip up his bag. I hear the door squeak open and catch closed, and McCallister is gone.

*

On the way to the car, the day too warm for January and the sun too strong for my mood, I know there is only one place for me to go.

Five hours later I arrive in Moab, the red rock cliffs

aglow with the remnant sun. I find Ford half-submerged under his shingled trailer, his boots scraping the parched mud ground.

"Hello?"

He shimmies himself out from under, and dirt-smeared and hair askew, leans against the cinder-block foundation.

"Well, well, well," he says, pushing his hair from his eyes with his wrist. "Welcome to Moab."

He holds up his greasy hands and I pull him to his feet.

"Why don't I fix us dinner and you can tell me all about it," he says.

He takes my hand and I follow.

*

As Ford serves up the rice and beans, I tell him about my night with Sam Gomez.

"Oh, Jane," he says.

"I'd gotten really complacent about the danger. I started to think I really was doing a good thing."

He comes around the little table and takes a seat next to me.

"He told me to be a good sport," I say. Ford winces but then we start to laugh despite ourselves.

"I guess this means I quit," I say. "And now, I don't know." I take a huge gulp of beer.

"I'm glad," he says.

"Little by little you make compromises and allowances. You're just answering the phones, then you're only stripping—hey, it's legal, it's not such a big deal—and then it's just your body and it makes someone else happy. Pretty soon you wake up and you are doing things that you would have never deemed okay."

"I assume the 'you' in this scenario is you," he says.

I laugh. "It's that obvious?"

The wind has picked up outside, and through the window there is nothing but dark.

"How are you anyway?"

"I'm just fine," he says.

"I saw Ember," I say.

Ford nods and reaches for a tortilla.

"She's planning on going to Spain or some grand plan like that."

"That sounds like her," he says.

"I imagine she left your heart pounded to smithereens."

"Yeah, but on some level I knew that there was no clear patch of sky just around the corner. I knew it was never going to be right."

He rises for another beer.

"Who am I kidding?" he says, kicking the refrigerator shut behind him. "I was flying blind. It sucked when she left. It still sucks."

We laugh.

"That's why I like Moab," he says. "I know how it all

works here. I don't need a constant readjustment."

"McCallister showed up," I say.

"In Utah?"

"On my doorstep."

"It's not all that surprising," he says.

"This time I broke up with him."

"You're better off," he says.

I lean my head on his shoulder.

There is scratching outside the door, then the sound of gnawing. I turn to Ford.

"Porcupines," he says. "They like the taste of shingles."

＊

Ford leads me on a tour of the homestead. We walk behind the trailer and stand at the edge of a moonlit gulch, listening to the snow-melt stream below. Ford puts his arm around my waist and we walk together, matching steps.

"On Christmas I went to see this old man who'd had a stroke and couldn't talk," I say. "When he fell asleep, I discovered his darkroom in the backyard with boxes and boxes of the most beautiful still life photographs. There were no people in any of them, nothing living, except for a few shots of his atrophied hand. The pictures made me so sad, all hidden away."

Ford stops and looks up for a second.

"I don't think that's sad at all," he says.

He turns and walks backward, facing me. In a nasally Willie Nelson imitation he begins to sing.

"I looked to the stars, tried all of the bars, and I've nearly gone up in smoke. Now my hand's on the wheel, of something that's real, and I feel like I'm goin' home."

chapter 22

Salt Lake County District Attorney David Lochman said his office decided not to file charges against a man who allegedly attempted to rape an escort service worker because jurors would believe the act had been consensual. "You can't say she was hired and paid big money to go to a man's motel room to do lewd dances for him in the nude and then come back and say she was attacked after she has been paid twice the original amount," Lochman said.

—*Salt Lake Tribune*

I feel like I owe it to Mohammed to resign face-to-face, so when I return from Moab, I drive over to Premier.

The office is as it always is: dim, faintly smelling of coconut oil from the tanning closet and the artificially floral after-scent of the big purple candle. Kendra is on the phone, reciting her well-rehearsed, flirtatious pitch while she reads her horoscope in *Glamour*. It's only 10:30 in the morning but she sets up some new girl whose name I don't recognize for a date at Little America. Kendra's eyes widen at the sight of me and she waves with one of her red-taloned fingernails.

"I thought we'd seen the last of you," she says when she hangs up.

"Where's Mohammed?"

"Next door," she says. "So is that it for you, Roxanne?" Kendra asks.

"Yeah, I think so," I say.

Although the rug store appears closed down—it doesn't even have a sign—the door is open and the bell rings as I enter. The square room is filled with thigh-high stacks of Oriental carpets in various sizes, lushly colored and intricately patterned. I want to bite into the cardamom browns, the honey golds, the berry-stained crimsons. I feel tradition and artistry all around. I lift up a corner of a rug, only to find the next one just as impressive. I can't believe I've never bothered to come in here before. I had no idea of the bounty.

I hear the swish of Mohammed's suit before I see him.

"May I help you?" he asks in an obsequious tone. "Oh. It is you."

"Hi," I say.

"So," he says.

"I guess you figured out that I quit."

He picks at a thread on the edge of a rug. "Yes, well.

You are not the first."

"Did you see the paper today? What the D.A. said?"

"I do not want to talk about this," he says. "I am tired, you know? I am thinking about getting out of the business altogether."

I raise my eyebrows.

"I am not doing something right. It is more headaches, less money, all the time."

"You know what I think?" I ask.

"I do not believe I have a choice in that matter."

"You have an untapped gold mine right here," I say, patting a stack of rugs.

"It loses me money too," he says.

"Because your visibility is bad, you don't advertise, and you're running back and forth so much, even your hours of operation are spotty. I had no idea what you had here and I've been only one door away."

"Well," he says. "What would you propose?"

"Why not concentrate your efforts. Spruce up your image, get a Web site. Really make a go of it," I say.

"Hm," he says. "I will think about this."

His cell phone rings and he has a quick conversation in Arabic. He gets up and heads toward the back. But then he stops.

"You know what my motto is?" he asks.

"I can't begin to imagine."

"You cannot always be happy, but you can always fill your eye with beauty."

I think of the photographs of the tree stump, the egg, the work boot.

"I stole it from George Hamilton," he says.

"The tan guy?"

"The same. *Love at First Bite* was the first movie I saw in America. I have been a big fan ever since."

*

A postcard arrives today from Ember from Telluride, Colorado. "We got a little sidetracked," it says, "but heading up to Portland soon. Then Spain and olé, baby!"

When I was in Moab, Ford told me that when Ember was eight and living in a shabby apartment in Milwaukee, she and her brothers had a plan to take a raft down the river and sail away. So they saved all the change they could, stole some, filched from their father's pants—until they had amassed the twelve dollars for a mail-order inflatable raft with oars. Her mother had been gone for days on a bender and her father was out scrounging for work, so Ember waited for the mailman every day until the package arrived. The kids took turns blowing it up, and then on an overcast summer day, the five of them— the oldest only ten—set out for the river. They slid down a trash-strewn bank, holding the little red and yellow boat above their heads, before getting in the water.

They flowed with glee along with the current. Even though none of them could swim, Ember said she wasn't scared. At first no one noticed the bobbing raft with five children in the middle of an industrial river. But soon people were lined up along the bank, pointing in horror as the kids careened ever closer to the drop-off they had no idea existed. It was only when a helicopter arrived above them and ordered them to hold on to the line did they suspect they might be in some trouble.

The phone rings and it's Kendra.

"I know you said you aren't going out anymore but I have this guy who's insistent on not seeing anyone but you and I thought I'd at least ask. It's Scott, that one you all say is hot."

It gives me pause to imagine meeting Scott over coffee, coming together like old friends. Flirting. A first date and a last date. A bit of cinematic symmetry.

"I don't think so," I say. "Tell him I moved away or got married or something. Or whatever. Tell him what you want."

*

In September 1857, in a meadow in southwestern Utah, a militia of the Church of Jesus Christ of Latter-day Saints attacked a wagon train of Arkansas families bound for California. After a five-day siege, the militia persuaded the families to surrender under a flag of truce and pledge of safe passage. Then the Mormons slaughtered 140 men, women, and children. Only 17 children under the age of eight—the age of innocence in the Mormon faith—were spared. The church first blamed the massacre on the

Paiute Indians, then, as evidence mounted, on a Mormon zealot and militia member who was also the adopted son of the prophet Brigham Young.

"But of course it was church leaders who ordered the massacre," Ralf says. "The poor bastards thought they were doing God's work by ridding the world of infidels."

I ran into Ralf this morning in the Coffee Garden for the first time since our winter picnic, and now, over biscuits and gravy at Ruth's, he and his purple-haired girlfriend Luna are fervently explaining to me their campaign to get the church to own up to its past.

"Mormons are fanatical documenters of history. They like to say there's a record of everything. So of course they know," he says.

"The church refuses to admit LDS leaders had anything to do with the massacre," Luna says. "And without any attempt to atone for it, it's a history built on dishonesty."

"We're trying to set things right, even if it's 150 years late," Ralf says.

"My band does a song about it," Luna says. "You should come to our next show and hear it."

"I'd like that," I say.

Their affinity for each other is bright and heartening.

"We're going down to Moab in a couple weeks to visit Ford," Ralf says. "I'm trying to convince him to come up to do this job with me in Murray that starts pretty soon. It'll be cake. Just painting. And it's inside."

I laugh. "It'll be just like old times."

"Something like that," he says.

Luna rests her ring-laden hand on Ralf's forearm.

"Ralf and I were in the same ward as kids. Same church and everything. Then I saw him a couple of months ago for the first time in like fifteen years. He looks the same as he did when he was twelve," she says.

"You know how people say things happen for a reason?" Ralf asks. "That used to really bug me because what they're really saying is there is a "good" and God-sanctioned reason for bad things to happen, and that reason is necessarily okay because it's part of God's grand plan. Anyway. After finding Luna, I'm not annoyed anymore."

"How come?" I ask.

He shrugs. "Because I'm happy."

*

Jezebel disappeared. It took a while before anyone believed it. The first few shifts she missed at work and the unanswered phone messages were nothing new for her, so no one thought much of it. Finally Nikyla went by her apartment and there was some old man living there who said he'd just moved in. When Nikyla found the landlord he said Miss Smith had owed three months in rent and she had had an illegal dog so he finally had the locks changed. But it didn't really matter, he said, because he never saw her again anyway.

It happens all the time in this business, girls just vanish without a word. There was never a good-bye or an explanation from Jezebel. Now there is just a void. Nikyla thinks she ran off to L.A. with some guy she was sent on a date with.

I look for Jezebel while I'm walking around the city even though I know it's futile. I hope she didn't latch onto something or someone worse. It's amazing to me that vibrant and girlish Jezebel could be lying in a morgue drawer and I would never know. Then again, she could be on a beach somewhere, still working on her tan, still contemplating her rise to stardom, as her boyfriend waves to her from atop a surfboard and Albee frolics in the sand.

I thought escorting would get me closer to the bottom of real life. But as Nikyla said, "It is what it is. People with people. It's nothing to feel bad about. Even if it's something we'll never do again."

I'm having dinner at Saharan Sands, Mohammed's restaurant, for the first time. Nikyla is meeting me here for a celebratory dinner. She is probably the only escort in history to give two weeks' notice. I feel like I'm back on the other side of the line, looking in instead of looking out. I'm no longer privy to what goes on a few doors down at Premier. No one calls me Roxanne.

Up close, Mohammed's wife looks tired around the eyes but she is prettier than I'd thought from just seeing her through the window, her features delicate and composed. She is, surprisingly, very pregnant. Even if I might look familiar to her, I imagine she blocks out her husband's other business. She doesn't consider that I might be one of those girls.

On my last day in Moab, Ford took me on a hike in Arches National Park, up the smooth rock hills, through the chasms, and along the narrow pathways to the monolithic spires and ridges, and the gravity-defying red sandstone arches. The unlikely formations are bold, graceful, daring, without real purpose. Under the dwarfing span of Delicate Arch, against an endless blue expanse of sky, I felt lighter than I have in years. Ford said he thinks people like to find places that remind them of their fragility. He took my picture under the famous arch but he had to stand so far back to get the whole thing in that I'm not sure I'll be recognizable.

Nikyla, her skin perfect and radiant, sits down across from me smelling of vanilla and soap. She grabs my hands across the table.

"I'm so glad you called. I have such a craving for falafel," she says.

I raise my water glass.

"To the end of your escorting career," I say.

"*Our* escorting career," she says and clinks my glass. "You're not going to move back to New York now, are you?"

"I promised my friend Ford I wouldn't give up yet on Utah."

"Good," she says. "I want you around to babysit."

The thing about Utah is that despite its wholesome veneer, I've come to see it as it is, to know it in my way, and it's a lot messier and more alluring than it appears on the surface. And the truth is, I don't need a promise to Ford to keep me here. I can now say, yes, given the options, I choose to live here, to pitch my tent in this place that's seemingly far away from everything. For now, anyway.

I'd forgotten that when Marisa isn't answering phones at Premier, she comes here to belly dance. Over the stereo speakers, a pulsing drum-and-cymbal beat precedes her, and she sways out from the kitchen with no introduction, just the tinkling beads of her costume as her hips snake in tiny figure eights. This is the first time I have seen her dance, and Mohammed is right, her hips have a life of their own. Nikyla lets loose a catcall and the men at the table next to ours put down their forks to focus on the dancer. They are hooked. I smile encouragement at Marisa but she doesn't seem to notice.

epilogue

I got a letter a few weeks ago from Ember. She never made it to Spain. She eventually ended up back in Milwaukee, where she's been trying to stay clean. She lives with her mother, who's also on the wagon, and waits tables at a diner. If she has a boyfriend, she didn't mention him. Milwaukee, she said, is still the pits.

Mohammed closed Premier Escort because of an unsavory audit and, I like to think, my influence. Some of the escorts went over to Baby Dolls. None of us ever heard from Jezebel again.

Nikyla married her boyfriend just before giving birth to a baby girl she named Spencer. They now live in a sunny little apartment not far from the mall where she and her husband are both managers. I take Spencer every couple of weeks so her parents can go out on Saturday night—they're finally old enough to get into Club DV8. Spencer has silver studs in her ears, perfect chubby legs, and Nikyla's green eyes. I like to take her on walks through the shady evening streets of the Avenues.

Mohammed hired me to manage his rug store, since renamed Pasha after his new daughter. We've secured a lease on a new space with a much-needed front display window and good foot traffic up near the university, next door to the King's English bookstore. Our Web site has been up and running for four months and we've already shipped orders from as far away as Hawaii. I've been pestering Mohammed for a raise, and although he hasn't granted it yet, he did give me a gorgeous burgundy Persian carpet that now covers the floor of my living room.

Ford is finally moving up to Salt Lake for good. He has accepted a job as an avalanche forecaster and he's coming this weekend to look for an apartment. He's keeping the trailer in Moab—his country house he calls it—for frequent visits.

This is my second fall in Utah. Outside my kitchen window, the cottonwoods are orange, the walnut trees yellow-green, and the scrub oaks red on the mountains. Despite the drizzle, the colors are electric. On Saturday, Ford has promised me a hike out in Little Cottonwood Canyon, where the autumn chill will be settling in around the mountains and the yellowing aspen leaves will be aflutter in the wind like thousands of tiny clapping hands.

acknowledgments

My love and gratitude go to Alex Darrow, Jennifer Sey, Jane, Ron, Ronny, and Susannah Meadows, Darin Strauss, Mark Sundeen, Elisabeth Weed, Kate Nitze and the whole incomparable MacAdam/Cage family, Jessica Darrow and Mike Koehler, Peter, Kathy, and James Darrow, Meredith Bell, Lance McDaniel, Lynn Kilpatrick, Carolyn Frazier, Jeff Roda, Christopher Sey, June Cohen, Tricia Tunstall, Anika Streitfeld, and the girls who inspired this book.

I am forever grateful for two life-changing teachers, Lewis Buzbee and David Kranes. I would also like to thank Karen Brennan, Katie Coles, and my fellow writers of the MFA/PhD program at the University of Utah.